ONE-MAN WOMAN

Never again would Jennie let a man invade her feelings, only to shatter the equilibrium of her life, the way Max had done so cruelly. In future she was going to concentrate on her very pleasant job as a television make-up girl, and leave men severely alone. But how long would she keep her resolve, once she had met Derek Hunter?

ONE-MAN WOMAN

BY

JESSICA AYRE

MILLS & BOON LIMITED

15–16 BROOK'S MEWS
LONDON W1A 1DR

All the characters in this book have no existence outside the imagination of the Author, and have no relation whatsoever to anyone bearing the same name or names. They are not even distantly inspired by any individual known or unknown to the Author, and all the incidents are pure invention.

First published 1982
© Jessica Ayre 1982

Australian copyright 1982

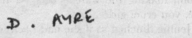

ISBN 0 263 10168 1

Set in Monophoto Baskerville 10 on 11 pt.
07–1182 – 60515

Made and printed in Great Britain by
Richard Clay (The Chaucer Press) Ltd,
Bungay, Suffolk

CHAPTER ONE

JENNIE LEWIS stood back to look at the face beneath her. It had put on years in minutes. She gently added another furrow to the brow, drew a few more pale, crinkly lines around the corners of the mouth. Then she dabbed some blue-grey cream under the eyes and rubbed it in delicately with her fingertips.

'I think that's it,' she said. 'You can look now.'

Daniela Colombi raised her head and opened lustrous eyes wide to look into the brightly-lit mirror.

'*Madre mia*!' Her shriek pierced the quiet of the dressing-room, making the walls echo. 'What have you done to me, you cruel girl?'

Jennie flinched as if she had been hit.

'My instructions were to age you by some thirty years,' she controlled her voice, 'and I've done just that.'

'You've done it too well,' Daniela Colombi muttered. 'I look older than my mother—*per Dio*, my grandmother!' She grimaced into the mirror, tried a smile, then a frown, and sighing, reached for the slightly scruffy grey-streaked wig perched on a dummy's head at the corner of the dressing table. She pulled it over the transparent plastic cap which covered her own luxuriant curls and gazed at her reflection. Suddenly a deep throaty laugh broke from her. It so jarred with the newly wrinkled face and thin-lipped mouth that Jennie too found herself giggling.

'You're brilliant, my Jennie, brilliant!' Daniela Colombi turned and patted Jennie's smudged hand. 'I must only swallow my enormous vanity and get used to my new self.' She got out of her chair, and then catching herself, sat down again and repeated the gesture more slowly, as if arthritis had suddenly gripped her joints.

5

Then she gave Jennie a sly wink, smoothed down the shapeless black dress which added pounds to her curves, and shuffled slowly towards the door.

Jennie watched the Italian actress in amazement mingled with admiration. Beautiful, voluptuous Daniela Colombi had turned into a suffering, shabby old woman. Reaching for a glass of tepid water, Jennie breathed a sigh of relief and sank into the nearest chair. She wiped a bead of perspiration from her brow and allowed herself a moment's rest.

They had been shooting for some weeks now and the pace had never slowed. It was Jennie's first major television film job. The cast and production team were of international repute and despite herself, Jennie was secretly thrilled. Her initial trepidation at working with stars had faded as she quickly fell in with the smooth professionalism of the rest of the team. Only Daniela Colombi presented a problem, and the make-up supervisor had assigned her specifically to Daniela. It had taken Jennie a little time to get used to Daniela's open shows of temperament, her rapid and violent shifts of mood, her outspokenness. She was quite unlike any actress Jennie had worked with before. Her blatant vanity, her quick-witted digs if everything wasn't just right, made Jennie nervous. Yet the actress's genuine warmth, her ability to vent her feelings immediately and loudly, had grown on Jennie.

So unlike me, Jennie thought as she pulled herself to her feet. She put together the creams, crayons, powders she would need for touching up between takes, washed her hands, drying them carelessly on her slender jean-clad legs, and strode out into the studio.

Once again the labyrinthine complexity of the vast space took her by surprise. A warren of constructed interiors—some with ceilings, some without, always with their fourth wall missing, like little makebelieve rooms in a doll's house. Yet lifesize, and set off from each other by lanes filled with soft-ware: cameras, monitors, lights. If she raised her head she saw a tangled web of girders and beams from which outlandish instruments projected, like some intricate spacecraft from the year 2500. It was all strangely hushed, lifeless, despite the seemingly random movement of people, the echoing sound. Until suddenly, with the clack of a clapperboard, lights and actors brought one room in the maze, one particular set, to life.

The commotion at one end of the large hangar-like space indicated to Jennie that they hadn't yet started to shoot. As she approached, she noticed Daniela Colombi at the centre of a noisy group. Among them were Matthew Tarn, the bulky good-natured English director; and his Italian assistant, Piero Sraffa, quick and elegant in his movements. Towering over the others was the scriptwriter, Derek Hunter, his blue gaze unseeingly directed at Jennie.

Jennie stopped in her tracks until Daniela waved her insistently towards the group. 'Come, Jennie, you're the one they should be congratulating, not me. I'm simply your creation.'

Jennie felt a flush rising to her cheeks, as Daniela urged her to the centre of the hubbub. She hated being conspicuous and she stood there uncomfortably, shifting from foot to foot, as the other woman acknowledged her handiwork.

'Let me tell you something,' Daniela Colombi looked at her conspiratorially and stage-whispered. 'They all secretly prefer me this way.' She cast her oddly wrinkled luminous eyes over the group of men. 'The all-embracing peasant *mamma* they never had—and too old to challenge them!' She burst into an infectious laugh which stopped short as she met Jennie's eyes. 'Oh, I'm embarrassing you, *cara*.'

Jennie shook her head a little stiffly. But she was grateful that Matthew Tarn chose this moment to call them to work. She briskly inspected Daniela's face, then turned toward a chair at the far end of the set. Just as she was moving out of earshot, she overheard Daniela say, 'So solemn, these English girls. What's wrong with you men? Can't you bring a smile to her lips?'

Jennie felt herself flush again. She was relieved that she was now all but invisible to the rest of the crew, and could watch their co-ordinated activity from a safe distance.

A hush fell over the set and as the clapper boy shouted out, 'Scene 212, Take 1,' an old peasant woman busied herself with scrubbing the stone floor. Despite the intrusive floodlights, the movement of the cameramen, Jennie was transported to a Sicilian kitchen, only to be rudely thrust back into the present by a shout, 'Boom!'

Jennie shook her head and smiled. It had never ceased to amaze her that with all this sophisticated technology no one had ever devised a sensitive microphone which didn't need to be held on a long pole over the set and inevitably cast its shadow on something or someone. Now the scene had to be started all over again. Jennie laughed to herself. Daniela couldn't often have scrubbed floors, but she did it with an air of practised authenticity.

The distinct impression that a gaze was moving up her spine and fastening itself to the nape of her neck startled Jennie back to reality, and she turned abruptly to look over her shoulder and the make-up kit fell off her lap, clattering to the floor. Jennie groaned and simultaneously heard the director's exasperated, 'Cut. Can we have quiet over there, please?' She murmured an apology, picked up the kit and moved noiselessly back to her chair.

A featherlight tap on her shoulder almost made her jump out of her seat again, but she controlled her movements, only lifting her face slightly. Yes, she had been half prepared for the face she would meet—Derek Hunter's. His sea-blue eyes had left their imprint on her before, but she was unprepared for the frank intimacy of his gaze now, as his fingers lingered on her shoulder and he mouthed a soundless, 'Sorry.'

Jennie gave him a withering look, jerking away from his touch and fixing her eyes deliberately on the set in front of her. But it wasn't so easy to rid herself of the sense of Derek Hunter's presence. She had noticed over the weeks how behind the coolly relaxed, the friendly façade, there was a fierce energy, an almost reckless determination. It showed itself in the sudden flare of his nostrils whenever there were arguments over even a detail of the script; and he inevitably got his way. Jennie had also observed that even the apparently fearless Daniela was a little in awe of him, listening carefully when he went over the script with her or made directorial suggestions, and looking for his approval between takes.

She felt her eyes now drawn toward him. Covertly she caught the outline of his long legs stretched carelessly in front of him, the movement of a hand through a thick mass of burnished hair.

'Cut. We'll take that again.' Matthew Tarn's voice was the signal for Jennie to move into action. She walked towards Daniela, aware of Derek Hunter's soft tread just behind her, and then matching hers.

'Sorry about all that before.'

'Oh, it's all right.' She kept her voice cool, impassive.

'Can I take you out for a drink tonight to make up for it?' He made her turn to face him and she looked up to see a humorous glint in his eyes.

Jennie shook her head, relieved to hear Daniela's voice calling her. It saved the necessity of finding excuses.

'Come quickly, Jennie, I think the years are melting off!' Jennie hurried to repair the wrinkles and creases on Daniela's face, and Derek followed.

'Are you two, how do you say it, hatching something together?' Daniela looked at them quizzically. 'I warn you, Jennie, don't steal my boy away from me.' Daniela had taken on her character's plaintive croon, but Jennie detected an undercurrent of seriousness in her tone, a knife-edge of menace, and it surprised her. Was there something between Daniela and Derek Hunter? She spent so much effort keeping herself to herself that she hadn't noticed. Yet the thought troubled her a little. Daniela, she knew, was married, or had been married, to a famous Italian producer. Their union had been prominent in the press some years back. But perhaps . . . Jennie chased the fruitless speculations from her head and busied herself with pencils and creams. It was, after all, none of her business.

For some time now Jennie had deliberately steered well clear of all relations beyond the professional. She had put behind her any thought of close friendship, of men, of anything that would intrude on her private life. A chill ran through her as she pushed the reasons why from her mind and concentrated on dabbing a little powder on Daniela's nose.

Derek meanwhile had taken Daniela's cue and was improvising a little comic scene.

'Oh, Mamma, how could your little boy leave you yet? He's only approaching middle age and desperately needs you to look after him. Like all good boys.'

Daniela gave him a playful kick and relaxed her face into Jennie's hands. 'That one, Jennie, is a dangerous man. He pretends to be all kindness and light, and underneath he's like granite. One has to take a hammer to him.'

'Mamma always knows best,' Derek joked, but his deep wide-set eyes as they momentarily met Jennie's over the unseeing Daniela were strangely cold.

Matthew Tarn strolled over with Arno Sati, the gentle, somewhat weatherbeaten actor who was playing Daniela's husband in later age. 'Almost ready, Jennie?'

She nodded.

'Good. And no accidents this take, please. I want to finish on time tonight, not only to save pennies, but so that we all get a proper break over the weekend.'

Jennie bridled at the rebuke, but said nothing. Derek's eyes were on her again, charged with an insistence which was almost palpable. She tried to still the slight quiver of her hands and moved quietly away to the far edge of the set, hoping he wouldn't follow her.

A question from Arno kept him with the others as they once again paced out the movements for the scene. Jennie watched him from her safe distance: the tall, broad-shouldered, firm body, tensed, yet with an athlete's agility, was somehow incongruous with what she knew was a keen intelligence. She had heard him briefing the cast at the beginning of the film, and his perceptions on Italian history and current politics—not a subject she was in the least familiar with or indeed particularly interested in—had captured her imagination.

It was odd, too, that he seemed to be playing such an active part in the shooting of the film. In her year's experience of working on television plays, she hadn't yet encountered a writer intervening quite so much in the filming. The word was that directors normally kept them at bay, worried that there might be arguments, concerned that actors and cameramen didn't receive two separate sets of instructions and grow disgruntled. Yet Derek and Matthew worked well together, bantering, discussing, one happy to accommodate the other's ideas.

Over the year Jennie had grown to love the work she had taken up only in order to keep skin and bone together. When things were going well during filming there was a sense of camaraderie, a team spirit which was quite unique in her lonely life. But she continued to keep herself separate, to guard her apartness. There was too much she felt she had to hide, and any intrusion on this self-enforced privacy might topple the fortress of order she had struggled so hard to build. Never again would she let a man invade her feelings, only to shatter the equilibrium of her life. Meanwhile, she realised, she was almost happy.

'Cut!' Matthew's voice and the sound of the clapper

broke into Jennie's reflections. She hurried to see whether Daniela's face needed touching up. Matthew was giving instructions to the cameramen and lighting technicians to reshoot part of the scene from a different angle.

Jennie had been astounded at how slow and repetitive filming was. Each brief take could be repeated countless times until the tedium was resounding. Yet there was also an excitement to it all, a rising tension tempered only by replays of the scenes on the monitors, when they were using video-cameras.

She applied some light greyish powder to Daniela's face, took a hurried look at Arno and moved quickly out of the way. She was the only make-up woman on the set for the moment and she didn't want any more rebukes from Matthew or glances from Derek. Thinking of him, she had the distinct impression that she could once again feel his eyes on her. Her hand moved unconsciously to the nape of her neck and turning her head a little, she saw that he had followed her to her place at the edge of the set. He gave her a slow questioning smile and sat down next to her.

Jennie focussed her eyes on Daniela and Arno, watched the flow of their gestures and voices as they acted out the scene. Daniela was really remarkably good. Jennie could hardly believe she was the same woman who had walked into the studio that morning. And it wasn't only her new face or her clothes, but the way she had matched each motion to the character.

'All right, everyone, let's call it a day now.' The floor manager's voice rang out across the studio as he relayed Matthew's instructions from the monitoring room above. A hum of conversation and activity sprang up from all sides. Jennie got to her feet to go and help Daniela remove her thick make-up, but a restraining hand held her back, and she turned round and found herself face to face with Derek, her eyes level with the soft material of his shirt taut over broad shoulders. He placed a finger under her chin and lifted her face to meet his. Jennie lurched backwards away from his touch and collided with Jim, the chief sound technician.

'Sorry,' she muttered, feeling ridiculous.

'Are you sure you don't want that drink?' Derek asked, the insistence of his eyes belying the humorous tilt of his lips. 'It might steady you.'

'You'll be lucky if you can get a yes out of this lady,' Jim intervened drolly. 'I've tried for months—offered her castles in Spain, dinners at the Savoy, glittering diamonds, even myself. And still she said no.' Jim shook his head in mock despair. 'But perhaps she'll respond to your greater charms.' He flashed them both a smile and sauntered off.

'Difficult, are you?' Derek looked her up and down with evident curiosity.

'Perhaps I am,' Jennie flung at him, her embarrassment tinged now with anger. 'And the answer is still no.' She strode off to the dressing room, letting her long legs carry her as quickly as they could without breaking into a run.

In the dressing room, Daniela had stripped off her wig and was rubbing her face with cold cream. 'I thought I might try going out in the streets with this old face just to see how people responded, but I lost my nerve.' Daniela grimaced despondently. 'I depend on men's glances far too much. I need them to confirm that I exist, exist beautifully. Not like you, eh, my modest little wildflower? Untouched by the eyes of men.'

Jennie shrugged. When she thought about it, she realised that she spent much of her time trying to be invisible. But untouched? Involuntarily, her hand moved to the nape of her neck and she felt the imprint of Derek's look. She ripped Daniela's plastic cap off with unusual force and watched the richly auburn curls tumble about her face and shoulders.

Daniela caught her eye in the mirror. 'I've made you angry, Jennie. I'm sorry. It's this big mouth of mine—everything comes spilling through it. But I'm right, no?'

she curved her full lips into a pout. 'You forgive me, yes? and when we finish this film, I'll make you up. You'll see, you'll be even more beautiful than you are now.'

Jennie smiled at the flattery. Daniela herself was irresistible as she preened her newly-found face before the mirror, applying her own richly red lipstick and just a hint of pink to her tawny cheeks. She pulled off her shapeless black garment and donned her own dress, a loosely flowing pale green silk gathered by a wide belt at the waist.

Jennie looked admiringly at the returned Daniela Colombi. A little shorter than Jennie, more generous in her curves, she exuded an earthy warmth which made Jennie feel pale and insignificant. Yet she couldn't resent her: she was so very much *there*, so open with herself and to the world.

Releasing her thick black hair from its few grips, Jennie glanced cursorily at her own reflection. The long dark mass now framed her finely chiselled features and emphasised the ivory of her skin. It also made her look absurdly young, like a schoolgirl grown tall before her time.

She passed a brush quickly through her hair, wished Daniela a good weekend and turned to leave. As she opened the dressing room door, she all but bumped into a man's figure. Derek. He stood there, hand raised, about to knock. She brushed past him, managing a curt nod, and then walked away. Behind her she heard him proclaim sardonically in a loud voice, 'The standard of common courtesy in this business is sadly on the decline.'

Jennie hurried blindly out of the studio, pausing only when she was well out of doors. A light drizzle fell from the early evening sky. She reached into her large shoulder bag for her denim jacket, pulled it on and fastened it securely all the way up to her neck. Then she went in search of her bicycle at the far corner of the car park.

Why on earth did I behave like that? she chided herself, her ears ringing with Derek's comment. Up until now she had managed to sidestep advances from the men at work in a friendly if shy manner. There was little point in making enemies, even if avoiding close contact was a priority. But with Derek Hunter her casual mask had slipped.

She waved to the guard at the television centre gate and wove her bicycle through the traffic. Pushing the recent scene from her mind, she concentrated on riding, not a simple matter on wet roads at this time of the evening, but quick and economical. And once she reached quieter streets, she loved the sheer sense of the wind in her hair, the joy of swift, self-powered movement.

She left the pleasant streets of Chelsea behind her and crossed over Battersea Bridge, enjoying the play of lights on the Thames. Her flat was just over the river. As always, she approached it with a slight anxiety. She brought her bicycle into the hall, looked around quickly, but no, there was no dark figure looming. She breathed her relief, locked the bicycle securely and went up the two flights of stairs to her flat.

Before unlocking her own door, she knocked at the one opposite and called, 'Everything all right, Mrs Owen?' She heard the sound of slow shuffling footsteps and waited. The door opened on the latch and a pair of bright blue eyes peered out of a lined face.

'Hello, dearie, have time for a cuppa?'

Jennie nodded and watched Mrs Owen's trembling fingers rise to the latch and open it clumsily. Mrs Owen smiled a warm greeting. 'Have a good day, dear?'

'Very good,' Jennie answered, and crossed the tiny room to take her place on one of the chairs at the wobbly kitchen table. Mrs Owen lived quite alone and Jennie knew that she depended on her visits as almost her only form of companionship.

When Jennie had first moved into the flat opposite last year, the old lady had shyly invited her in for tea. Aware of her loneliness, her diminishing strength, Jennie had taken to visiting her regularly, looking in to see if she were all right, or stopping to chat. Then in the course of the year she had begun to help the old lady with her shopping, bringing in groceries, making sure she had an adequate supply of tins. When she had painted her own flat, Jennie had discreetly suggested that Mrs Owen would like to make use of her remaining paint and she had proceeded to cover Mrs Owen's gloomy walls in glistening white.

Jennie realised that her neighbour would have rejected anything that smacked of charity. But she genuinely liked the old woman, her fierce determination to carry on alone as long as she possibly could, her occasional flashes of wry humour. She also knew that in her own way she too depended on the old woman's presence. Mrs Owen was perhaps the only person in London who would notice if Jennie vanished: more importantly, Jennie thought, a mild self-pity stirring her, the only one who would care.

Mrs Owen pushed a wisp of white hair away from her forehead and chuckled as Jennie told her how she had turned the beautiful Daniela Colombi into a near replica of Mrs Owen. Then, having drunk down the last of her tea, she took her leave, promising to call in tomorrow with a supply of groceries.

She crossed the hall and opened the door to her own flat. Switching on the light and looking around her, she was once again struck by her good fortune. The room which faced her wasn't vast, but its large bay window looked north on to a row of trees between which she could see a green and catch glimpses of the river. The flat was a front one in an old mansion block which had seen better times, yet it was one of the few London flats where rent was controlled. Off the main room, there was a small bedroom and a tiny kitchen. Jennie had worked hard on the place, stripping down layers of mouldy wallpaper, constructing kitchen cabinets and shelves and painting the

whole in a sparkling white which made the rooms grow in
dimension. The carpentry skills she had developed gave
her almost as much pleasure as the finished product.

She dropped her bag on the sofa she had made out of
two foam mattresses and brightly-coloured fabric and
went to stand in front of the easel in the window recess.
She examined the figure on the canvas closely, her fingers
itching to start work on it again. Tubes of oil paint covered
the small table at her side. Under it Jennie had constructed cabinets in which her paintings could stand.

It was painting that was Jennie's real passion, but she
had quickly realised during her first year at art school
that there was no way she could support herself simply by
doing that. The choice was to join the ranks of commercial
artists or do something else. She had decided, for several
reasons, on the latter, doing a course in stage and film
make-up and leaving what painting talent she had free
for serious work. Now every spare minute she had was
devoted to painting. Since she couldn't frequently afford
models, she roamed the city with her sketch pad looking
for interesting faces, doing rapid drawings which she could
take home and possibly rework on canvas. The painting
which stood on the easel now was that of a young boy,
hair spiky green in punk fashion and eyes which looked
sadly out to a lost world. But the expression of the eyes
was in sharp contradiction to the taut jerky lines of the
body poised for assault. Jennie looked at the painting
carefully, seeing where she would have to add colour,
mute outlines, blur shape. She picked up a tube and then
dropped it abruptly. Food first, she had promised herself.
She often forgot to eat when she was home alone, and
Daniela Colombi's comments on her thinness had made
her determine that she would do so regularly and
healthily.

Jennie took a chop out of the small refrigerator, placed
it on the frying pan with some herbs and peeled two large
potatoes which she set to boil. Waiting for her food to

cook, she turned on the radio. A news report on Italy drew her attention. The crew would be travelling there soon and though Jennie was usually loath to leave her flat and her painting, she looked forward to this first trip abroad with excitement. Sicily: the name itself was magical, bringing with it the scent of orange blossom, visions of trees laden with olives, with lemons, and the grimmer aura of a criminal Mafia.

Now the urgent tones of a partisan song poured out of the radio.

> *Avanti popolo alla riscossa,*
> *Bandiera rossa, bandiera rossa.*
> *Avanti popolo alla riscossa,*
> *Bandiera rossa trionferà!*

Yes, Jennie remembered, this was one of Daniela's tunes, something about people moving forward to rebellion, the triumph of the red flag.

She picked up a wooden spoon, threw her shoulders back, and tapped her feet to the rhythm, her long hair swinging. How good it was to have a place of one's own, to do whatever one pleased, far from others' eyes and tongues. How wonderful to relax, not to have to put on a face to meet the faces of others. Freedom. Jennie found herself in front of her green-haired boy. A wide smile breaking over her face, she put down her spoon and picked up a fine brush. The smell of burning meat seemed to disturb her not at all.

CHAPTER TWO

THE morning sun shone brightly as Jennie left her flat the next morning. The sky was a limpid blue, the clarity of the air seemed to outline each apple green leaf, each cornice, each railing separately. Jennie took a deep breath. Spring had come at last. Spring, Jennie chuckled at the direction of her own thoughts, when a young woman's fancy turns to . . .

Taking a firm grip on the sketchpad beneath her arm, she decided to walk rather than cycle. It would take her a good hour to cover the distance, but what bliss to be able to see London free of its grey, winter drabness. Even the faces, Jennie remarked as she sauntered along, seemed to have changed overnight. Gloom had broken into smiles, people seemed to be looking outward rather than in.

She crossed the river, walked along the Chelsea Embankment, pausing only once to do a quick sketch of an old bearded derelict stretched out on a newspaper-covered bench. Then she wound her way through the imposing streets of Belgravia past the Wellington monument towards Green Park.

Paintings and crafts already covered the railings of the Park, framing the green of grass and trees outlandishly. People milled round, chatting, looking, buying. Children tugged on fathers' hands, asking to be carried on shoulder top or demanding merrily-coloured balloons. Piccadilly had forgotten its everyday existence, the rush and scurry of missed appointments, and taken on the air of a bazaar.

Smiling, Jennie walked through the Park gate and looked round for a few moments. She made her way towards a small circle of people who seemed intent on a

single object. Yes, she had been right. There, in the centre
of the group, sat Colin, perched on a stool, his head bent
in concentration. He was applying blunt charcoal strokes
to a sheet of paper. Miraculously the strokes joined together to form the face in front of him. Jennie watched
the deftness Colin brought to his task. His jet black eyes
hardly ever seemed to touch his subject. It was as if he
had taken the face into himself at a glance and now
seemed to be drawing from memory.

His drawing finished, Colin looked up and caught her
eye. A slow smile spread beneath his bushy black moustache and he nodded, gesturing towards the railing where
he had propped two folding chairs. Jennie fetched them
and set them up at a small distance from him. She took
her box of pastels and another of charcoals out of her
copious bag, set up a few sketches around her, and while
waiting for custom she began to sketch Colin.

The two had struck up an easy friendship some time
back while Jennie was still a student. She had come to the
Park with great regularity then, needing the extra money
that the quick portraits brought in, as much as the practice. Gradually, she couldn't quite remember how, she
and Colin had singled each other out and struck up a
loose bantering twosome. They worked close to each other
in the Park and Colin, who had a small van, had offered
to transport Jennie's chairs for her. She had expressed her
gratitude, and he had grinned, 'I'm the one who's grateful. It makes a change to have some worthy competition
around here. My work improves.'

'What competition?' Jennie remembered chuckling
wickedly. 'You get all the young lovers, almost all the
attractive women, and all the men. Mothers and children
come to me, and then only sometimes.'

Colin had replied sternly: 'Subjects are irrelevant in
this part of the work.' But he had smilingly acknowledged
that she was right.

And she had been more right than she knew, Jennie

now realised as she sketched the long line of Colin's arched back. In all the Saturdays and Sundays she had spent in the Park, she could count on her two hands the instances when a man who wasn't well past his prime had sat before her. It was as if they were afraid that sitting passively to be drawn by a woman would rob them of some intrinsic strength.

She shrugged and noticed that a woman pulling a small girl by the arm had emerged from the group who had gathered round her. The woman made the girl sit in the chair opposite Jennie.

'I'd like you to do a portrait of her for her grand-mother's birthday.'

Jennie nodded and smiled into the little heart-shaped face with its slightly frightened round eyes.

'It won't hurt,' she said, 'and I shall try to make you just as lovely as you are.'

The little girl rewarded her with a smile and tried to sit still. Only one swinging leg indicated her nervousness.

Jennie drew the small face quickly, shaded in the slight flush of the cheeks, the smooth wide brow. 'There,' she said. 'Come and tell me if you like it, and if you don't, I'll do another.'

The small warm body came close to hers and scrutinised the picture. Then the round eyes looked up at her.

'Could I do a picture of you now?'

Jennie laughed at the child's audacity and handed her the box of pastels and a sheet of paper. Very seriously she drew Jennie—a figure sitting stark upright in a chair, strands of hair all but covering big black eyes.

'There,' said the little girl. 'You can keep that and put it up here next to the others.'

Jennie did so and handed the little girl her portrait. 'A fair exchange,' she said, glancing up at the mother, who wasn't sure whether to be embarrassed or proud.

Jennie went back to her sketch of Colin. His face en-grossed her. She felt she could never quite catch the austerity of its expression, somehow give life to the determinedly solitary aspect of his character. In it, she thought, there is a clue to myself. Colin, like her, was quite happy to be friendly, but only up to a point. There was a part of him which remained intensely private, almost secret, and although they had shared drinks and chat and she had even gone to his studio once, the veil of secrecy persisted.

She wondered whether he had a family ghost in the closet. The thought made her shudder as it brought the image of her own all-too-obtrusive ghost with his shaming presence.

Sensing a shape in the customer's chair, Jennie looked up, and surprise made her drop the pastel in her hand. There in front of her was Derek Hunter. His arms comfortably crossed, his feet firmly planted on the ground, a glint of irony in his smile, he appraised her coolly, and Jennie felt her pulse quicken.

'Hello, Jennifer Lewis.' His voice was gruffly humorous. 'So this is what you do with your time!'

Jennie returned a slightly breathless hello and bent to pick up the dropped pastel. As she worked to compose her face, she realised that there was anger just beneath the surface of her surprise.

'What are you doing here?' she asked curtly.

'I've come to have a portrait done of myself for my grandmother's birthday.'

He's mocking me, Jennie thought, seething inwardly. She controlled her voice. 'There's a man over there,' she gestured towards Colin, 'who's a far more experienced portraitist than I am.'

'Oh, I've shopped around,' Derek said lightly, 'and I've decided on you.'

'The subject doesn't interest me, I'm afraid,' she managed icily.

He arched a single eyebrow and gave her a long slow look. 'I didn't realise one could dismiss subjects quite so perfunctorily in the Park.'

Jennie stifled a brusque reply, and swallowed hard. 'All right, I'll do you. For your grandmother.'

She rejected the pastels in favour of charcoal and jabbed at the paper with unwonted ferocity. The line she had drawn, she realised, had nothing to do with his face. It followed the angular jut of his shoulder through his shirt. She relaxed a little, allowing her hand to be her eye.

Small rough strokes traced the shape in front of her. She looked up and met Derek's gaze. He was staring at her acutely, as if he were the artist, not she.

Yes, Jennie thought suddenly, that was why men wouldn't on the whole pose for women. It reversed all suppositions, both about art and life. Drawing Derek, she was actively possessing him, shaping him, while he had to remain at least momentarily passive. She traced the angular line of his jaw, the oddly sensual lower lip, the wide somewhat feline eyes, and then, meeting them, realised he was resisting her, still watching her vigilantly. She smiled to herself, rising to the silent challenge, and made the eyes in her portrait wary, yet strangely ardent, as if they wanted to do the seeing without themselves being seen.

The result was discomfiting and not quite achieved. Jennie memorised the picture and moved to tear it up. It would need more work in the quiet of her studio. But before she could crumple up the drawing, Derek was at her side, stopping her hand.

'No, no, I'm paying for this pleasure.' He gripped her wrist with strong fingers and looked over her shoulder. Jennie flinched away from him, but her wrist remained locked in his grasp.

He looked at the drawing for what seemed a long time. 'Yes, you're right,' he said in a low voice turning his blue eyes fully on her, 'I do desire you.'

Jennie struggled to escape the insistence of his voice, his eyes, his hand on her wrist.

'Is this gentleman disturbing you, Jennie?' an icy voice

at her side dispelled her rising tide of dizziness, and she turned to see Colin standing protectively by her, his dark eyes focussed threateningly on Derek. Still keeping hold of her wrist, Derek stood his ground. Only when Jennie had found her voice and uttered the 'no' dictated by common sense did he gently release her.

'Colin, meet Derek. We work together,' Jennie mumbled an explanation.

Colin looked at her questioningly, as if searching for the truth of her words. Then he glanced briefly at the rumpled drawing in her hands, at Derek, and again at the drawing.

'Interesting sketch, Jennie,' he said limpidly.

Derek chuckled, 'I've been trying to prevent her from destroying it. By rights, I assume it's mine,' he dug into the pocket of his trousers, 'at least once I've paid for the commission.'

Jennie gave him a scathing look. 'It's not for sale. I don't sell unfinished work. Your grandmother,' she added, suddenly finding a mocking tone, 'will just have to be satisfied with another present.'

Colin eyed them both quizzically for a moment. 'I'll leave the two of you to sort this out.' He gave Jennie's shoulder a light pat. Then laughing, he added, 'Shout for help if your model—or is it your patron?—turns nasty!'

Jennie tried to still the quiver of her hands as she felt Derek's now suspicious gaze on her.

'I guess my grandmother will have to wait until the drawing is finished,' he said at last. 'But *my* patience isn't quite so well developed. How about having that drink with me? Or a spot of lunch?'

Jennie tried to think calmly. There really was no way of extricating herself gracefully from the situation. And she did after all have to work with Derek. She would somehow have to be friendly, but assert her distance. She steeled herself to it.

'Yes, why not?' She raised her dark, thickly-lashed eyes

and tried to meet the blue of his gaze evenly.

Derek smiled his pleasure. 'You don't know what this does for my dwindling ego! I'd all but given up hope. And another "no" after this morning's trek from Battersea would have all but ruined me.' There was a mocking tilt to his lips.

Jennie felt the blood ringing in her ears. 'You mean you followed me here?'

He chuckled, 'The studio didn't seem to have a telephone number for you, only an address. So I turned up and . . .'

'You followed me,' Jennie finished abruptly. A shudder ran through her as the idea of being followed unknowingly through the streets came home to her.

'Mmm. I quite fancy myself as the hero of a thriller. Brazen detective follows mysterious lady through tangle of London streets. Mysterious lady, who by all known reports refuses castles in Spain, invitations to the Savoy, tantalising diamonds. And says "no" with conviction.' Derek laughed, but catching the troubled look on Jennie's face, he stopped.

'I'm sorry if that upsets you,' he said in a low voice. 'But it's not only that I'm insatiably curious. I did want to see you.'

Jennie shook off the warmth of his glance and bent to gather chairs and sketches. Derek took them from her and followed her towards Colin.

'I'll be back in a little while, Colin,' Jennie said, feeling somehow embarrassed.

Colin glanced up from his drawing, nodded and waved her off. Beneath his breath she thought she heard him say, 'Take care of yourself, little one.'

And so I will, Jennie remarked to herself. But as she felt the warmth of Derek's fingers on her arm, guiding her through the crowd, a tremor of doubt passed through her. Perhaps it had been a mistake to diverge from her ritualised no. She shook herself mentally and braced her nerve.

'What shall it be, my mysterious dark lady? A glass of white wine and some smoked salmon to welcome the spring? Something a little more substantial?'

Jennie shrugged and looked down at the old jeans she had tucked into her high boots in preparation for cycling through the city; her loose white smock shirt. 'As long as it's not the Connaught Hotel. I didn't think to bring my tie.'

Derek grinned and straightened an imaginary knot at his throat. 'My attire, on the other hand, is impeccable,' he drawled.

Jennie noticed that the jeans, stretched smoothly over his long muscular legs, were as worn as hers, his sky-blue shirt was open at the neck. Unwillingly too, she took in the tautness of his stomach, the curly gold-brown hair which escaped from the open button of his shirt, the strong tendons of his surprisingly bronzed neck. A disturbing thought flashed through her mind. What a wonderful nude study he would make! The flush crept into her cheeks as she tried to put the idea aside. But it persisted.

Of course, that was it, Jennie suddenly determined. Attack was the best line of defence. She would treat him as the subject for a painting. Coolly detached interest; a clinical distance. The strategy appealed to her. It was the only possible one with a man who wouldn't take no for an answer.

They crossed over Piccadilly and he led her through a small shop-clustered lane, down a few stairs to a wine bar. As Jennie's eyes grew accustomed to the interior dimness, she made out comfortable wicker chairs and tables with glass tops, couples engaged in a low hum of intimate chatter. Derek pointed out a back table by what appeared to be a small glassed-in courtyard. Potted palms framed a tiny sunken pond.

Jennie sat down and waited. Within a few moments she saw Derek coming towards her carrying a bottle of white wine and two glasses. He moved through the crowd with a cat's grace. No, Jennie corrected herself, more like a tiger waiting to pounce. A smile came to her lips as she remembered her resolve.

He caught it. 'I see I've earned myself momentary grace,' he said as he eased himself into the chair beside her.

Jennie attacked, 'I was just thinking what a delicious subject you would make for a nude study.'

She saw him visibly stiffen. Then he met her, his eyes suddenly fiercely black beneath his rugged brow. 'I might offer my services,' his voice was light in contradiction to his gaze, 'if I thought the artist were good. Have you done a lot of male nudes?'

Jennie blanched. 'Not very many,' she lied, knowing she had done none from the life, terrified that he might take up her offer.

'I don't know how Grannie would respond to a present like that,' he reflected, the mockery coming back to his voice.

Jennie was saved from replying by the appearance of the waitress carrying plates of smoked salmon and brown bread.

'I'd better wash my hands,' she said, grimacing at her charcoal-smudged fingers. She walked quickly to the ladies' room, washed and looked at herself in the mirror. Did she look different, she wondered, now that, as Daniela might have said, she had been touched by the eyes of a man? The same straight nose, slightly too wide mouth, thickly-lashed brown eyes beneath well-defined arches. Yes, there was a strange sparkle in their brown depths. Jennie bent her head and let her hair fall over her face as she combed its length savagely. Why on earth this ludicrous self-examination just because a rather arrogant man had followed her through the streets? She threw her head back and let the waves of her hair fall where they would over her shoulders. Determining that she would end this meeting soon, she walked back towards the table.

Derek's eyes were insistently on her as she moved across the room, and she felt her skin tingle as if caressed. It was a new sensation and she lowered her eyes, unwilling to meet his.

He filled her glass and lifted his to her. 'To our first drink, no mean achievement in this case.'

Jennie bit back her, 'To our last,' and took a large gulp of the chilled wine.

'Do you paint as a hobby?' Derek asked.

'Do you write as a hobby?' Jennie countered before she could stop herself.

'Touché!' He looked at her with interest. 'But I don't hide it. Why the secrecy? No one on the team has mentioned it to me.'

Jennie shrugged. 'It's no one's business but mine, is it?' The hostility in her voice was a little too evident. She tried to steer the conversation back towards safer ground, but with those eyes fixed on her, her mind was a blank.

'No,' he chuckled, 'you're quite right. There's your work and there's your life. And you want me to stop interfering in the latter, right?'

Jennie nodded, still avoiding his eyes.

'But writers are curious animals, Miss Jennifer Lewis. They have to *know*. It's an incurable urge, and in this case it's directed at you. So tell me something about yourself, or I'll just have to keep on following you.'

Jennie shuddered, forcing herself to meet his eyes. They were in deadly earnest, unlike the playful tone of his voice. The air between them was so charged, it was difficult to keep her voice steady.

'Jennifer Lewis, born Leeds, age twenty-two, height five foot six, weight, somewhere around eight stone; profession, make-up girl; aspiration: painter. Will that do, Mr Writer-Detective? Or would you like my National Health number as well?'

He laughed and a twinkle appeared in his eye. 'I would have thought seven stone was more like it. But I see I'll have to take up your modelling offer if I'm to find out any more.'

Jennie could feel her knees turning to water, but she managed a reply. 'Given the way our director is working us, I'm afraid I won't be able to use you until some time in the future. Why not leave your number with me and I'll get in touch.' She rose to go, but he put out a hand to stop her.

'There's still some wine in the bottle. Why not finish it?'

'I should get back to work, or should I say, to my hobby?' she said coolly.

'In the trade I think this is what they call the brush-off,' he looked at her intently, forcing her to meet his gaze. 'Or am I wrong?'

Jennie felt a glimmering regret rising in her, combined with a stronger impulse to flee. Her voice was thick when she found it. 'I don't know,' she said honestly. 'But I do know I have to go.' She attempted a polite nod, a thank you, and all but ran through the wine bar.

At the corner of the street she paused to catch her breath. Her heart was pounding as if she'd just experienced a narrow escape. I've gone quite barmy, she thought to herself. Sitting having a drink with a man, and I act as if my life were at stake!

She took a deep gulp of air and walked slowly towards the Park to retrieve her things from Colin. He eyed her astutely. 'Decided against him, have you, Jennie?'

'I'm afraid so.' She tried to sound casual.

'Well, it's back to the old easel. Shall we have a painterly chat tonight over a bottle of wine to quiet your nerves?'

Jennie shook her head. 'I'd like to, but I'd better get back home now and do some more work. There isn't much time left until I'm off to Italy.'

'Rain check until you get back then. Buck up, girl. That was a good drawing you did of your Derek.'

'Hardly my Derek, or my idea,' Jennie shrugged, 'but thanks.' She smiled warmly into Colin's dark eyes. 'I'll see you in a few weeks.'

She watched for a while as Colin tossed off a sketch of a young Chinese woman and then proceeded slowly through the Park.

'Do you mind if I walk with you rather than behind you?'

Jennie almost jumped out of her skin at the sound of the deep voice at her side. Derek was matching his long paces to hers.

She shrugged.

'I left my car in front of your flat,' he offered by way of explanation.

'The pavements are free,' she muttered ungraciously. 'And I can't very well stop you.'

A note of anger came into his voice. 'Perhaps I'd better tail behind you after all. The view seems to be better than the company.'

She shrugged again. 'The choice is yours.'

He said nothing, but he stayed beside her, his gait rhythmically linked to hers. Jennie looked blindly straight ahead. All pleasure in the fresh spring day had left her. Her mind was a jumble of irrational fears which fused into only one clear thought: how would she rid herself of Derek once they had reached her flat? His arrogance seemed to be such that a straightforward no made no impact whatever, and she couldn't, just couldn't chance the possibility of that all over again. She felt dizzy with the pressure of it.

A hand on her shoulder made her flinch.

'Let's stop a minute, Jennie,' Derek said, making her turn towards him. They were on the Embankment and he guided her towards the river's edge. 'Are you living with someone? Is that it?'

'No,' she blurted out honestly, and instantly wished she'd said yes. It would have solved everything.

'Well, what is it, then? I don't repel you, do I? Attraction, I've learnt over the years, is usually a two-way street.'

She looked up at him, taken aback by his straightforwardness. No, he was hardly repulsive; too attractive if anything, with those wide-set deep blue eyes in that rugged bronzed face. Her look must have betrayed her thoughts, for a mocking gleam came into his eye.

She shrugged, finding an odd high-pitched voice somewhere in herself: 'I simply want to be left alone.'

A low rumbling laugh emerged from him. 'I've hardly asked you to share my life with me; a drink, a little friendly conversation, perhaps something else.'

Jennie caught his eyes roving over her face and across her body. She turned away abruptly, slinging her sketch pad across her chest and holding it there firmly with both arms crossed over it as she strode away, head held high.

He was beside her again in a moment and continued as if there had been no interruption to their talk. Only the note of mockery was stronger in his tone now.

'The funny thing is you don't strike me as a man-hater, nor an ardent feminist. God knows, I've met plenty of those—and of the most virulent kind—in California. There are two sorts, I decided. The first simply want to be men—why, I haven't quite been able to figure out; we're hardly wonderful. They want to be men not only in their relation to the world of power, but in their sexual habits. Love them and leave them. It seems to agree with them even less than with men of that kind.'

He paused, waiting for some kind of response. When Jennie said nothing, he shrugged. 'Well, I don't think you're like that. Then there's the other kind. Full of plans for social reform. Women's equality, equal opportunity. I'm all for it, even help where I can. It's the humourlessness for the approach which is so stultifying. Though inevitable, I suppose. I haven't met too many social campaigners of either sex who are particularly endowed with wit. Still, when the earnestness intrudes into everyday relations, I groan. I can't really see why it's necessary.'

'If you'd listen to yourself for two minutes, you'd see why in a flash,' Jennie lunged out, surprised at her own vehemence. 'You're patronising beyond belief!'

He chuckled wryly, 'A response at last. I'd almost lost hope.'

Jennie flushed and kept a tight grip on her hands. She felt she would like to give him a good hard slap. Instead she quickened her pace.

'You're right, of course,' he said a few seconds later, his tone serious. 'I'm being insufferably smug, passing judgement. But, you know, we're all beginning to treat each other like walking specimens of a gender. It's the differences between men and women that are important to me, the differences between each single one of them that I'm curious about.'

Jennie suddenly laughed. 'Well, if you're following me because you're doing research on the nature of women, forget it. I'm not interesting enough. And I'm sure you've got quite enough candidates for a sociological survey without adding me to the list.'

'It's hardly sociology I was thinking of,' he muttered, his eyes searing into her.

They were nearing Jennie's door now and her sense of panic returned. She looked round furtively, trying at the same time to think of an appropriate goodbye. Derek noticed her discomfort.

'Don't worry, I won't force my attentions on you.' He looked at her questioningly and passed a finger lightly down her cheek. 'Too bad, though. We might have been good together.'

Jennie's cheek burned, holding the imprint of his touch. Impulsively she put out her hand. He took it and held it, his long fingers enveloping hers. 'No hard feelings,' she said, a question in her assertion, and then added inconsequentially, 'I think your script is marvellous.'

He laughed, still holding her hand, a sardonic gleam in his eye. 'I'm so very glad you approve of something about me.'

Jennie flushed. She tried to extricate her hand from his, but before she could do so, a voice called from behind her.

'Hello, Jennie, I thought I'd just come down for a breath of spring air.'

'Hello, Mrs Owen.' Jennie shook off Derek's hand. 'What a good idea. Shall we take a little stroll together?'

Mrs Owen looked at Jennie and at Derek, and a wide smile crinkled over her face. 'Oh yes, Jennie, but I wouldn't want to disrupt your plans.' A comic archness crept into her features. 'Aren't you going to introduce me to your young man?'

Jennie blanched and then controlled her voice. 'This is Derek Hunter, Mrs Owen. I think I mentioned to you that he wrote the script of the film we've been working on. Derek, this is my neighbour and friend, Mrs Owen.'

Derek took Mrs Owen's hand. 'I'm pleased to meet a friend of Jennie's.' The irony of the comment was meant for Jennie alone. Mrs Owen was obviously impressed by the politeness of tone.

'I'm sorry if I intruded.'

'Oh no, on the contrary, it would be my pleasure if we could both accompany you on your walk.'

Mrs Owen beamed, and Jennie groaned inwardly. A sudden excuse occurred to her. 'Er—Mrs Owen, I quite forgot the shopping. Why don't you stroll with Derek while I do it, otherwise the shops will close.'

Derek intervened, 'We could take the car and all do it together.'

'That's really not necessary,' Jennie parried. 'The shops are just down the road.'

Mrs Owen's word was the final one. 'It would be rather nice to walk down together. Then Mr Hunter could help us bring the packages home.' Mrs Owen smiled sweetly and Derek returned her smile with warmth, giving her his arm.

They set off slowly down the street.

'This is very convenient, Jennie. We had wanted to get rather more supplies in than usual, since you'll be off for a while.'

Jennie conceded the point, nodding sweetly, but fuming inside. Mrs Owen would be sure to invite Derek in for tea, and somehow that would lead to an invasion of her territory. She trembled with apprehension.

Meanwhile Derek chatted pleasantly to Mrs Owen and gave her his arm. Jennie glanced at him from the corner of her eye. He seemed to be totally engaged in the conversation. Not a note of condescension was visible in his voice as he told Mrs Owen the story of the film. He met her glance for a moment and a flicker passed through his eyes, but then he seemed to lose interest in her altogether and gave his whole attention to Mrs Owen.

They walked into the local supermarket, and Derek casually reached for a trolley. 'Lead the way, ladies. I'm at your disposal.'

'How very kind,' Mrs Owen smiled her thanks, and she and Jennie busied themselves with selecting provisions. Jennie felt herself relax a little as Derek's attention strayed from her. He appeared quite content behind his trolley and Jennie wondered a little at the time he seemed to be willing to give to so ordinary a task. Catching her glancing at him, he gave her a long slow wink and a wide smile broke over his face, as if he'd read her mind. 'It makes a change from the typewriter!'

His easy good humour was strangely contagious and despite herself, Jennie found herself smiling in return. But her smile stopped halfway. Daniela's words had suddenly popped into her mind: 'Hard as granite'. Difficult to imagine that now as he towered over Mrs Owen and explained to her why it was far better for her to be eating brown bread instead of white.

As they neared the check-out counter, Derek vanished for a minute, only to return carrying two enormous boxes of chocolates. 'My contribution to the provisions,' he commented wryly.

Jennie noticed the cashier gazing up at him with adoring eyes and then glancing at Jennie with new respect.

Women! she mumbled to herself contemptuously, judging each other by the partners they happened, perhaps randomly, to be with.

'Something troubling you, mysterious lady?' Derek murmured out of Mrs Owen's hearing as they left the store. 'And yet I've been on my best behaviour.'

'Not all my thoughts are linked to you,' Jennie found herself saying, barely veiled hostility in her voice.

'Oh, of course, how stupidly patronising of me to presume——' his tone was light, but the ferocity in his eyes made Jennie shudder.

They had reached the flats. 'You must both come up and have some tea with me now. It's the least I can do to thank you,' Mrs Owen's voice invited them kindly.

Derek glanced at Jennie, met her eyes, and shook his head. 'No, no, Mrs Owen, I really mustn't impose myself on you any longer. Besides, I should be heading back.'

Mrs Owen turned to Jennie. 'Do convince him to come up, dear, I'm sure he'll listen to you.'

Jennie tensed. She was being cast in an impossible role. But it would mean so much to Mrs Owen, a brief adventure in the midst of her lonely life. She forced herself to smile warmly. 'Do spare us a few minutes, Derek. Mrs Owen makes a good cup of tea.'

Derek took in the irony of the situation and his smile mocked her. 'Well, a few minutes won't, I guess, make much difference. My appointment can wait a little.'

'There I knew you could win him over, Jennie,' Mrs Owen all but bounced up the stairs to the door of her flat. 'Not very grand here, but it's ever so much better since Jennie so kindly painted it for me.' She looked gratefully at Jennie, who could feel the warmth of Derek's gaze on her.

They placed the groceries on the small kitchen counter and Jennie busied herself putting them away, while Mrs Owen brewed the tea and chatted gaily.

'I've always thought of writers as being pale and sullen and—well, superior,' Jennie overheard her say, and almost dropped the tin she was putting up on a shelf. 'But you're not at all like that.'

Derek chuckled. 'You must be confusing writers with painters, Mrs Owen.' Jennie cringed. 'But perhaps you're right. I'm just wearing my Californian mask at the moment.'

'California? Do you spend a lot of time there?'

'As little as I can. They don't treat their writers very well in Hollywood. But I was partially brought up there. My mother was American.'

Mrs Owen poured the tea into her best cups, put out some freshly bought biscuits, and opened the large box of chocolates Derek had given her. 'And your father?'

'English as they come,' Derek smiled. 'A great believer in the public school system—sent me off to one as soon as he could. Amazing really that I survived. But then it was back to the United States for holidays, or Italy, where my mother's side of the family lives. So I'm a bit of a chameleon,' he drawled, his accent broadening as he broke into American.

Jennie listened attentively. She had been so preoccupied with fending Derek off that she realised she knew almost nothing about him, except from professional hearsay.

'*Belle donne, mille grazie,* but I must be off.' Derek emptied his cup and stretched to his full height, dwarfing the tiny room even more. 'Thank you for a very pleasant afternoon.' His gaze lingered on Jennie for a moment, but his smile was merely polite, warming only as Mrs Owen urged him to come again, any time, and not only to carry groceries.

As she saw him vanish through the door, Jennie felt oddly hollow. A wave of disappointment surged through her. What had she expected? Mrs Owen's comments on the nice young man and so handsome, too, only served to irritate and she escaped to the solitude of her flat as soon as she could without hurting the old lady's feelings. She flung her sketchpad down on the sofa with unusual force and sat down beside it, pulling her high boots off her slender legs.

A restlessness overtook her. She paced the room, looking desultorily around her, and finally picked up the sketchpad to gaze at the somewhat crumpled portrait of Derek. Yes, what had she expected? That that look of desire should persist despite her offhand and even at times insulting manner? Shame crept over her, making a heavy pulse beat at her temple as she thought of her childish lack of graciousness. And what *did* she want? Derek in her room now, touching her with his hands rather than his eyes? No, not that. She felt her knees grow weak and she sank down into the sofa, a tremor passing over her. Surely not that? She had been right to rid herself of him in any way she could. It was his unusual persistence which had undone her, the sheer power of his gaze which stirred something unfamiliar in her. It had taken so much effort of will to give her life a semblance of order, and to allow it to be disrupted now, just when things were under control, was lunacy.

Jennie gave herself a mental shake, stood up and undressed slowly as she walked towards the bathroom. A shower—that was what she needed. She let the needle-sharp water pour over her slender frame, lathered shampoo thickly into her hair, washed it off and rubbed herself pink with a large towel. Then she walked naked into the studio room. Catching a glimpse of herself in the long mirror she had propped against the wall to help her see her paintings from different angles, she stopped to confront her own image. A delicately curved body looked back at her, its shoulders sheathed in black hair, a face insignificant in its finely moulded features, but for the wide dark eyes, now slightly haunted.

Jennie shrugged and pulled a dark blue towelling robe over her. This self-examination was puerile. She took Derek's portrait out of the sketch pad and pinned it up on one corner of an unused canvas. She looked at it steadily for what seemed like a long time. Then, almost like a sleepwalker, she prepared three colours. With swift, jagged brush strokes, she painted a glistening golden mask, hollow-eyed, its metallic hardness crystallising in the cruelly mocking tilt of its lips. Beside it, merged with it, a man's face, ruggedly warm, mellow with tenderness.

CHAPTER THREE

JENNIE slept fitfully that night. She woke late, feeling bruised, unsure of her whereabouts, the images of her dreams still hovering just behind her eyelids: masks—coldly gleaming, frighteningly wrinkled, ripely wanton, and sadly derelict, danced bodiless to hollow laughter around the face of a bemused, wide-eyed little girl.

Jennie rubbed her eyes and tried to stretch some life into her stiff limbs. Then she lay still for a few minutes remembering the previous day. Shame engulfed her once more. But she flung her blankets back and got out of bed. 'That's that!' she said out loud. 'Finished with. Pointless brooding. And the painting is going to be good.'

She wrapped her blue robe over her shoulders and made her way to the kitchen, pausing for a moment to glance at the work of the night before. A smile came over her face. It really wasn't bad. She should be grateful to Derek. A perky little tune came to her throat as she brewed some strong coffee and then sipped it slowly, savouring its rich flavour. Her second cup followed her to her canvas and stayed there, growing cold, as she immersed herself in her painting.

A knock at the door reminded her that she wasn't yet dressed. She drew her robe more tightly around her and padded barefoot across the room, fully expecting to see Mrs Owen's cheerful little face bearing Sunday greetings.

As she opened the door, she automatically looked down to where Mrs Owen's white curls usually were, but what confronted her instead was a stretch of worn denim. Jennie's gaze travelled nervously upwards to meet the sea-blue of Derek's eyes, and she jerked backwards.

'Sorry, didn't mean to startle you. But I thought I'd

take advantage of that nude portraiture today. Sundays
are so tedious.' His voice was light, but his eyes carried a
deadly seriousness. 'It's after twelve, you know,' he added,
taking in her dressing gown. 'I'm sorry if I got you out of
bed.'

Jennie's voice wouldn't surface. Derek's presence
loomed over her, charging the atmosphere of her flat with
what was almost a tangible danger. She gazed mesmerised
at his animal litheness as he walked past her into the room.
Finally she found her voice. 'I've been working,' she said,
hoarsely but evenly, and as an afterthought, because she
had to busy herself with something, 'Would you like some
coffee?'

He laughed. 'I think that's the first civil thing you've
ever said to me without prompting! I would be over-
joyed.'

Jennie ground some beans and made some fresh coffee,
trying to still her agitation. She could sense his eyes burning into her back.

'I'll just put some clothes on while this is brewing,' she
said, attempting lightness.

'Not much need, is there?' His broad chest blocked her
exit from the kitchen. 'If I'm to strip, I'd really feel more
comfortable if you weren't too properly clad.' He lifted
her face to meet his eyes and chuckled. 'Don't look so
frightened,' he touched her cheek lightly with soft lips.
'I'm not in the habit of assaulting women. Though you
do provoke one.' His eyes travelled down her slender
form.

Jennie brushed past him, unable to find any retort, and
went into her room, shutting the door firmly behind her.
Tears tingled at the backs of her eyes, but she held them
away. She could feel her heart beating a quickened
rhythm, her pulse racing. What was she to do now? She
pulled on yesterday's jeans and a fresh shirt and then,
unable to come to any resolve whatsoever, walked back
into the studio room.

Derek was looking thoughtfully at the painting on the easel. 'Perhaps you don't need me to pose after all,' he said as she came to his side. 'In all of this,' he gestured at the canvas, 'my physical presence seems somewhat redundant.'

She managed a laugh. 'Coffee? Black? White?'

He didn't answer. 'I don't know whether I should be flattered or dismayed. Flattered at having inspired something as good as this,' he paused, 'or dismayed at the way you see me.' He looked up at her. 'Black, please,' and then back down at the canvas. 'Dismay wins, I think.' He chuckled grimly. 'I don't think I dare trust my poor naked body to you after this. Your eyes would demolish it.'

She handed him his coffee. His hand brushed hers as he took the cup. She flinched and he caught her eyes.

'No, perhaps I will after all,' he said reflectively. With slow deliberate movements he placed the cup on the table and started to remove his jacket.

'No!' Jennie's voice was shrill. 'Not now.'

'I'm only taking off my jacket. It's warm in here.' His laughter was teasing. 'Yes, perhaps I dare after all. It would change your way of seeing.'

'I may just call your bluff.' Jennie met his tone, riled now at his obvious teasing, his implicit criticism.

He looked at her suddenly with deadly seriousness, his eyes measuring her as they travelled from her face slowly down her body and then back to meet her eyes again. She was aghast at the challenge she had unconsciously issued, and moved away from him desperately, feeling her knees buckle under her. As she reached the distance of the sofa and sank gratefully into it, trying with little success to keep her coffee from spilling, she heard him murmur almost inaudibly, 'Might you, now? I wonder just who's doing the bluffing.' Then, more loudly, in a voice tinged with irony, 'Whenever you're ready. Do I decide on the pose or do you dictate it? Or perhaps we should establish a little intimacy first. I'm told that's the rule between painters and their models.'

Before Jennie could find her voice, he was beside her, his strong arms lifting her out of the sofa, and crushing her shape to his. His lips sought her mouth with a wilful pressure. Jennie could feel herself drowning, suffocating in his embrace. Her fists rose to pound his back, his sides, his chest. 'Don't touch me,' the words emerged in a strangled sob.

Abruptly he released her. His eyes were black, relieved only by golden flecks, his lips drawn in a grim line. He pushed a hand through his thick hair. 'Not quite the intimacy I had in mind,' he muttered sardonically.

'Please go now.' Jennie's voice was icy in its quiet firmness.

He looked at her, meeting her eyes sceptically. 'Yes, I will, now.'

It seemed to Jenny that he took decades to pull on his jacket, reach for a pack of cigarettes in his pocket, offer her one, light one for himself, take a long slow puff and then walk towards her door. At the threshold, he suddenly turned. 'When you've stopped playing little girl games, mysterious lady, do let me know.' He nodded and walked away.

Jennie slammed the door behind him hard and rested her length against it. As her tensed body relaxed, sobs racked her. She went over to her bed and flung herself down on it, the tears streaming from her face. It had been so long since she had cried, really cried. And as she cried now, she could see herself as a little girl, huddled up in her bed in one corner of the dark room she shared with two others, trying to stifle her sobs so that no one could hear her. She had cried then, cried endlessly, every night until sleep overcame her.

The house had been a strange one, filled with the tumble of children who paid little attention to her but to tease her. Strong, oddly self-sufficient children, who seemed immune to pain. They were her cousins, she was told by a smiling woman who was apparently her aunt and who expected her to fit into the chaotic routine of the household with little ado. But she hadn't fitted in, not even when she had stopped crying and learned to smile; not even when she had learned how to create a small secret untouchable place within herself where no one could penetrate. It was this space in which she reserved her difference, her dreams, the first of which was to leave.

Jennie's mother had died when Jennie was seven, leaving her all but an orphan. Her stepfather, Harry, who had lived with them for only a year, had promptly deposited her at her aunt's in York and vanished. Her aunt and uncle, Jennie later realised, were kind enough, but what with four young children of their own, they had little special time for her. And the noise and bustle of the house had only made her draw further inwards, made her yearn for some kind of privacy.

Ever since she could remember, she had wanted to be on her own. To be on her own so that she could stop pretending to be like the others; to be on her own so that she could stop being grateful to this surrogate family who had taken her in. She had worked hard at school, even sometimes enjoying her studies despite the fun the other children had made of her seriousness. And it had been worth it. She had received a grant to go to art school in London where she had a place.

London had been like a burst of fresh air. All at once she felt she could be herself, share her interests, even though she had at first been terrified of her teachers, frightened of the sophisticated girls with whom she shared lodgings. By managing her money very carefully and saving her earnings from portraits in the Park, and by simple good luck, she had eventually managed to get her own bed-sit. The sheer joy of having a place of her own had made her buoyant. Life had seemed magically transformed. Wonderful.

And then she had met Max.

Jennie's tears had ebbed and she turned over on her back and looked at the blank whiteness of the ceiling. Max. No, she hadn't allowed herself to think of him for a long time now. She rose and went to her tiny bathroom, splashed cold water over her reddened face and looked at herself closely in the small mirror. It was after Max had left that she had begun to cry again.

Max was a lecturer at the art school, not all that much older than she was despite his seniority of place. He had taken an interest in her work, encouraged her. Then they had started going out for coffee or drinks together after sessions. Jennie had been amazed by his fluency, his knowledge of painting and the art world. He had talked to her for hours and she had listened breathlessly, taking it all in. One night he had told her to get dressed up. He would take her out for a proper dinner.

Jennie smiled as she remembered now the care she had taken to look well, digging into her savings to buy herself a new dress for the event, a brightly-coloured Indian print which set off her dark hair and ivory skin. He had taken her to a well-known Soho restaurant and wined and dined her regally. Then he had driven her home and asked if he could come in for a cup of coffee.

She had hesitated. Max had never been to her place before and somehow the thought of him in those close quarters filled her with dread. But she had acquiesced. They had talked and sipped coffee. And then he had kissed her, softly at first and later with growing intensity. Jennie had felt herself shrivel, grow slightly sick at his faintly acrid smell. Yet she hadn't withdrawn, hadn't quite known how to. He was, after all, the first man she had kissed and perhaps it was a business that took some getting used to. When he had left her, he had patted her gently, had said reassuringly it would be better next time.

Jennie had never had time for boys, never thought much

about them. All her dreams had been about leaving the
place she was in. If she thought about men and marriage
when the other girls talked of nothing else, it was all
somehow relegated to some distant haze of a future.
Meanwhile there was the task of escaping and setting up
on her own.

Max had been the first man to intrude on her enough
to leave an impression. She realised now, as she tried to
brush some order into her hair, that she had talked herself
into being in love with Max the man, in order not to
displease Max the teacher. And she had been in love in a
way: in love with the Max who talked about art, about
the ideal union between man and woman. Had been in
love except when he touched her. Then she retreated to
that small secret place in herself that she knew from
childhood. She had tried to return his kisses, don the mask
of attraction, but something in her had turned away in
faint repulsion. She saw it as a fault in herself which she
had to overcome. And he encouraged her to see it in that
way, making it quite clear that if she couldn't respond to
him, the lack was entirely her own.

One night he had said, 'Tonight's the night, Jennie.
It's time you were made a woman.' She had trembled in
fear, but had followed him dutifully to the sofa. He had
caressed her ritualistically and she had let him, retreating
to her small secret place. As his fervour had mounted, he
had gripped her fiercely, tearing open her blouse, kissing
her over and over with growing brutality. Jennie had
closed her eyes tightly against him and had lain there
coolly impassive, not knowing how to quell her repulsion
against this Max, so unlike the intelligent companion she
liked and respected. After what seemed an eternity, he
had sprung up in a rage, cursed her coldness, the way she
had, he claimed, led him on. Riddled with guilt at her
inability to touch the man she thought she loved, Jennie
stilled his anger by pleading with him that she felt unwell,
that she was frightened, tomorrow would be better.

But the next night had been, if anything, worse. Her body had rebelled against her will, against him, in cool repulsion. 'You're just a frigid little tramp!' he had yelled at her, straightening his clothes with angry movements. 'A useless, sexless creature.' It was then that the doorbell had rung . . .

Jennie shuddered and blocked the memory from her mind. She walked brusquely to the kitchen and poured herself a glass of cold milk, drinking it down in a rush. I need some exercise, she thought to herself, and fetching a jacket, she moved towards the door.

In the corridor, she all but collided with an enormous bouquet of flowers. Behind it stood Derek.

'Just in time.' He handed her the bouquet, his eyes glowing blue in his ruggedly bronzed face. 'With my humblest apologies,' he smiled at her warmly. 'I don't want you to go around thinking that I make a habit of forcing myself on defenceless damsels . . . even if they aren't quite defenceless,' he added wryly.

Jennie flushed, mumbling embarrassed thanks, and then as she unwrapped the bouquet on her way back into the flat, exclaimed, 'Oh, they're beautiful, simply beautiful!' A blaze of colours burst from the paper: daffodils, tulips, irises, anemones, stocks, masses of spring flowers, greeted her, warmed her. Her pleasure illuminated her face.

'I'm forgiven, then?' Derek took her hand and held it for a moment.

She nodded, feeling his fingertips burn into her and almost tighten her smile.

He looked at her appreciatively. 'With that smile, you're as radiant as the flowers. Until Italy, then.' He released her hand, a flicker of mockery on his face. 'I may not feel quite so humble in those pagan climes.'

Jennie watched him leave, gazed at his lithe walk across the room, and stood watching still as if mesmerised, after the door had closed behind him.

She roused herself to look for vases, bottles in which to place the flowers, and as she carefully arranged them to best effect, she was acutely aware of the imprint his body had left against hers, the searching power of his lips. Her hands shook and she hurried her task, placing the vases randomly here and there on all spare surfaces. Colour and scent filled the flat, transforming it into a springtime garden. Jennie looked around, reached for a jacket and went out, away from the presence the flowers embodied, intent now on the exercise she had promised herself.

She unlocked her bicycle and carried it out to the street. Then she pushed off, cycling randomly, letting the streets guide her where they would. It was another bright day and the sun gently warmed Jennie's back. The Sunday streets were almost free of traffic, so she allowed herself the luxury of breathing deeply. Some time back she had read of the disastrous effects of cycling in a city where the lead content in the air was disproportionately high. So she had tutored herself to breathe shallowly in traffic, knowing perfectly well that it made little difference. But today was special.

Finding herself in the vicinity of the Hayward Gallery, she thought she might have a stroll through the new exhibition of British art. Given that she would be away for a while, it might be her only opportunity to see the exhibit and she was curious to know what work the panel of notables thought worthy of exhibition. She rolled her bicycle along the Embankment, looking into the grey waters of the Thames. Children were busy on roller skates and skateboards performing extravagant feats to a casual audience of strolling spectators. Their antics enlivened the sombre concrete façade of the arts complex and almost made its heavy solemnity inviting.

Jennie parked her bicycle in a rack, then climbed up the winding staircase to the gallery. She bought a ticket and browsed for a few moments in the bookstall. A book on the future of modern art caught her eye. It would keep

her company on the plane journey, she thought, and purchased it. She then made her way slowly through the
exhibition. Oils large and small, some with visible figures,
others coded in the language of abstraction; constructions
of fabric, of wood, of aluminium; life-size plastic figures
encased in transparent balloons confronted her. Not much
that she immediately liked, but the sheer variety filled her
with exuberance. It was as if the panel had determined to
have one work of every kind, rather than trying to impose
some sense of a British school or trend on the exhibition.

She caught sight of some familiar brushwork and looked
more closely at the small oil in front of her. Max. He had
made it at last. Not very impressive, she thought to herself
as she studied the painting carefully. She chuckled, happy
to find that she could, and a little surprised that this con-
frontation with something Max had made should provoke
no turmoil in her.

Jennie walked on into the next room. At the far corner,
a strikingly handsome couple caught her attention: the
man, tall, broad-shouldered, with his arm protectively
round the woman's shoulders which were buried in a mass
of vibrant auburn curls. They stood so still Jennie thought
at first they might be one of the exhibits, placed so that
they could only be seen from behind. But as she approached, she saw the woman turn a languorous profile
towards the man.

Jennie stopped in her tracks. Of course, it was Daniela,
and the man she was looking up to with such a delicious
tilt to her chin was Derek Hunter. Jennie could feel a
tight knot forming in her stomach and moving up to choke
her. She made to retrace her steps, but it was too late. A
throaty voice rose above the hushed murmurs in the room.
'Jennie, Jennie, come and say hello!'

Jennie walked slowly towards the couple, trying to still
her speeding pulse. She put a bright smile on her lips and
kept it there tightly as Daniela moved to embrace her
and kiss her on both cheeks. 'How lovely to meet you by

chance like this! I didn't know you were interested in such things.' She made a sweeping gesture with her arm.

Jennie kept her smile bright and her eyes focussed away from Derek. 'Oh, but I am.'

She heard Derek chuckle. 'Didn't you know, Daniela, that Jennie is a painter?'

Jennie caught the mocking glint in his eye as his smile warmly acknowledged her presence.

'A painter? But, Jennie, that's wonderful! Why didn't you ever tell me?' She looked suspiciously from Derek to Jennie and back again. 'I'll never understand you English with your secret ways.' She shrugged her shoulders in exaggerated fashion. 'But now that you're here and I discover—a little late, *è vero?*——' she added wryly, 'that you're a painter, you might give us some professional insight into all this.'

Jennie tried to think of some valid excuse to absent herself. But it was hopeless. She knew that once Daniela had set her mind on something, there was no stopping her. Derek, she noticed, seemed to be enjoying her plight, her obvious embarrassment. A wide smile suffused his rugged features and his eyes twinkled mischievously.

'What can be better than one lovely lady but a second? Don't know how I'll concentrate on those pictures,' he grinned, 'though perhaps we might have a closer look at that rather voluptuous nude over there to fix my mind on art.'

Jennie's temper flared. She wanted to lash out at his contempt, but she stopped herself, suddenly thinking of a better ploy. If they wanted professional insight, they would get it until boredom besieged them.

'That "voluptuous nude"? Oh, but Derek, you're quite wrong, she's merely a traditional form, used here as part of a composition to balance the weight and density . . .' and Jennie proceeded to analyse the technical aspects of the canvas at interminable length. She could see the smile on Daniela's face growing rigid and then melting into a yawn, at which point Jennie stopped.

'Oh, I'm sorry. I can see I must be boring you.' She looked up at Derek, mischievous herself now.

'Not at all,' he countered, 'I'm thoroughly impressed. Couldn't have done better myself. God knows, at this rate I may even commission you to do a nude,' he paused significantly as Jennie felt a flush coming to her face, 'of Daniela here.' He put his hand on her shoulder.

'I'm not accepting commissions at the moment,' Jennie said icily.

'Oh, Derek, stop making Jennie uncomfortable. I'm sure she only paints what she wants to paint,' Daniela intervened, a distinct note of irritation in her voice as she took in the attention Derek was paying Jennie.

'I stand corrected.' Derek bowed with mock formality to the two women. 'May I treat you two ladies to some coffee as a sign of my good faith?' He threw Jennie a serious searching glance.

'No,' Jennie responded too quickly, and then tempered her abruptness. 'I want to see the rest of the show and then I have to get back.'

'I'm sure Jennie is busy with her own friends.' Daniela eyed her coldly. '*Arrivederci!* See you tomorrow, Jennie.' She turned to Derek and began speaking to him in Italian as he nodded goodbye.

Jennie walked as quickly as politeness permitted in the opposite direction. She felt dismissed, like an awkward schoolgirl, though the emotion made little sense since leaving had been of her own choice. Of course, it was clear to her now that Derek and Daniela were having an affair. The actress didn't hide it. And Jennie was the third, unwanted party, except for some momentary curiosity on Daniela's part. But then what was Derek doing following her, invading her with his presence, pursuing her? She stood absently in front of a vast canvas and grew hot and cold in turn as she remembered the pressure of his lips. Was that simple curiosity too for the writer-detective?

She turned on her heel, anger giving colour to her pale cheeks. The exhibition had been ruined for her. A plaything, that was what she was. The thought rankled and she strode unseeingly through the rooms and out of the door. Mounting her bicycle, she pedalled ferociously homewards. Work. It would be far better to work than to subject herself to all this.

She clambered up the stairs to her flat, still enraged. As she neared her door, she stopped and involuntarily let out a gasp. A grey bedraggled figure was hovering in the hallway. Jennie slowed her pace and tried to gain a grip on her nerves. Definitely not my day, she muttered to herself.

'Hello, Jennie, I've been waiting for you,' the form looked towards her. 'I thought it was time I paid my beloved stepdaughter a Sunday visit.'

Jennie cringed as the form planted a wet breathy kiss on her forehead. The sickly sweet smell of stale beer encompassed her.

'Hello, Harry,' she said, moving back a step and noting the falsely sentimental smile on the vein-cracked face.

'You're looking well, Jennie. Life at the television studios must be good.'

Jennie shrugged and opened the door to her flat.

Harry whistled as he preceded her through the door. He glanced at her slyly. 'Got yourself a new admirer, then?'

Jennie looked at the bright flowers which filled every corner of the room and smiled despite herself. She had forgotten about them and they were lovely. That, after all, had been kind of Derek.

Her stepfather took in her look. 'So I'm right, then? But no funny business, or I'll have to move in and protect you.'

The hint of menace in his voice was real, and Jennie forced herself to pay no attention to his comment. 'Would you like some tea, Harry?'

'Something more substantial, lass, if you can. I'm a trifle hungry,' his tone was pleading now.

Jennie nodded. 'I'll just ask Mrs Owen over and she can keep you company while I do the cooking.'

She closed the door momentarily behind her with a sigh of relief. She really was blessed to have Mrs Owen as a neighbour. The old lady had happened to come in once during one of her stepfather's unwanted visits and Jennie had noticed that she didn't seem to mind his company. She chatted on as sunnily as ever and it saved Jennie the trouble of being civil.

Jennie's stepfather had come back into her life some few years ago. She pushed the memory of the actual event hurriedly from her mind. His appearance had been totally unexpected. She had heard nothing of him or from him since that distant past when he had deposited her at her aunt's home. And then, all at once, there he was, a weak bullying man, often too full of drink, who had moved from odd job to odd job until nothing was left but the dole queue. It was then that the thought of his step-daughter must have come to his mind and he sought out Jennie's aunt to discover Jennie's whereabouts.

Once discovered, Jennie was at the mercy of his ir-regular visits. He would drop in about once a month, sometimes more, without warning. She would feed him and usually succeed in chasing him away only with a 'loan' which he promised to repay in some distant future. Jennie knew little about his life between visits and didn't want to know more. She felt this derelict of a man had nothing to do with her, but for the accident of his brief marriage to her mother so many years ago. In a childish way, she associated him with her mother's death; and though she occasionally pitied him, she dreaded his visits. He filled her with a deep, almost uncontrollable sense of shame, and she felt she would rather disappear altogether than have any of her professional colleagues see him as associated—however tenuously—with her. It was his presence she had grown to fear whenever she returned home, the one dark note in what had become an acceptable life.

Mrs Owen was only too pleased to make a visit.

'Oh, Jennie, duck!' she exclaimed as she walked into the flower-filled flat, 'how beautiful!—Mr Richards, isn't it simply beautiful, all these flowers?' she greeted Jennie's stepfather and paused by an overladen vase to sniff. 'Did you bring these for Jennie? No? Well then, I know exactly who it was. That handsome Mr Hunter,' she looked up at Jennie, a knowing smile on her lips. 'And so kind too.' She beamed at the two of them and around the room, her face crinkling into a thousand lines.

'You must have some to take back with you. There are far too many for this small space. I won't be able to breathe tonight.'

'Nonsense, dear. But if you insist I will have some, just a few,' she smiled her delight. 'No one has brought me flowers for a very long time.' She turned towards Jennie's stepfather and sat down gingerly at the edge of the sofa. 'Well then, Mr Richards, how has life been treating you these fine spring days?'

'Not so bad, Mrs Owen, not so bad, except for a touch of the old rheumatism.'

Jennie left them to exchange their traditional list of aches and went into her tiny kitchen. She took some bacon, eggs, and cheese out of the fridge and set herself to chopping up salad. The sound of Harry's voice from the next room set her nerves on edge. It never failed to, she realised, even when he was at his most charming and amenable. She chopped at an onion aggressively, feeling the sharp smell rise to her nostrils and prickle her eyes.

Suddenly the memory of that night came flooding back to her. It refused to be barred, to be blocked out in the way she had successfully managed for some time now.

She had been lying there rigid as Max reproached her, abused her, all the while tugging at his tie and pulling on his jacket with a frightening vehemence. The doorbell had rung just as he had finished placing his rimless spectacles on his nose. He had given her a scathing contemptuous look under which she could feel her skin shrivel and then he had marched straight out without so much as a glance at the stranger at the door with whom he all but collided.

Jennie had been too stunned to move as this bleary-eyed stranger approached her bed and began to rail in his turn. 'Fine goings-on for a daughter of mine!' he had shouted, and then proceeded to vilify her in language such as she had rarely heard. Jennie had been so confused, so frightened, that she barely had the presence of mind to tidy her blouse or ask who this stranger was. Then, gradually, as she had made this out from his jumbled monologue, her horror had mounted. She couldn't call for the police, she could hardly even bring herself to move, though she was panic-stricken as to what this man who called himself her stepfather might do in his obviously drunken state. So she sat there, as still as she could, waiting for the tirade to stop. And it did. After what seemed like hours, Harry had passed out on the tiny sofa. The next morning, he seemed hardly to remember what had happened, not even to be terribly clear as to where he was. His tone was humble and bullying by turns, and Jennie had finally rid herself of him by giving him some money and insisting that there was no way he could stay in the bedsitter without her being turned out.

She had gone off to classes like a sleepwalker, not knowing quite what else to do with herself. And when she had seen Max, he had cut her completely, not even acknowledging her presence. He had done so continually until Jennie could bear no more. Night after night, she cried herself to sleep. She couldn't believe Max's silence, the pain; and on top of it she dreaded her stepfather's imminent return, avoided going home until as late as possible. Her stepfather had taken on gigantic proportions in her imagination and a voice which in its railing was confused with the Max of that night. Together they formed a joint presence which derided her and blamed her.

Finally, after weeks of inaction, she had picked herself up, moved temporarily to a student hostel and looked around for a flat. She had stopped going to classes. The possibility of seeing this cold, strange Max who ignored her was too great. Not knowing quite what to do with herself, she had started helping out with odd jobs at a local fringe theatre where a fellow student worked.

She found in those long bleak months that she had a talent for make-up work and she determined to do it seriously. She also determined, though she never voiced it to herself as such, that she would take herself in hand; build some kind of order out of the shambles of her life and not allow anyone to intrude on her again. She had begun to insulate herself against men, taking Max, her teacher's definition of her frigidity to heart.

It hadn't been easy, but finding the flat had helped. And by the time her stepfather, Harry, had searched her out again, she had grown sufficient skin to face him. Though she still didn't invite anyone home, terrified that Harry might burst in during one of his drunken bouts and shame her irremediably. Apart from work, it had become a solitary life.

Jennie shuddered as she looked at him now over the small pine table which served as her dining space. No, it hadn't been easy. But the actual sight of him folding a large slice of bread hungrily into his mouth made her realise that of late she found him more pathetic than frightening. Though the habit of fear, mingled with a deep irrational shame, seemed to have become part of her, part of that buried secret self. Yet if she forced herself to think about it coherently, it was really Max and her stepfather who should feel the shame. It was at least in part they who had acted badly.

Yes, suddenly it all seemed a little clearer to her. Max's

total rejection of her, his resounding and bullying comments about her frigidity, had taken on a crushing force when compounded with her stepfather's drunken railing, the shame and fear he aroused in her. But was she frigid as Max had said?

She thought of the new sensations Derek's touch had stirred in her and her pulse beat faster. Or had she simply accepted Max's definition, generalised from one particular instance, and kept all men at bay because they might unearth this same quality of revulsion—and her unpresentable stepfather to boot?

Jennie shrugged inwardly. Finding the answer could well mean losing everything she had so carefully built up. She couldn't face a rejection as shattering as Max's had been again. She noticed her hand trembling as she poured the strong tea and willed herself back into the moment.

'What about a sweet, Mrs Owen?'

'Oh yes, dear. Why don't I fetch that large box of chocolates your young man so kindly gave me?'

Jennie refused, rising to unwrap her own box. As she passed the chocolates round, she glanced at the canvas in the bay window and Derek's eyes, those eyes full of mocking and desire which she had sketched only yesterday, met hers.

Yes, she would have to be very carefully on her guard to protect herself against that one, or everything she had built up would crumble.

CHAPTER FOUR

THE following morning the make-up room was packed with people. They were shooting the larger family sequences this week and since the film saw the family through three generations, there were not only minor characters to worry about, but Daniela and her film husband, Arno, to see to as well. Jennie and the two other make-up girls had their hands full.

Caught up in the bustle of activity, Jennie had little time to think. It was midweek before she became aware that her nagging sense of unfulfilled expectation was due to the fact that Derek hadn't turned up on the set. It was Daniela who brought it to her attention.

She was studying her middle-aged mask in the mirror—that of a statuesque, rather formidable matron who had saved her husband Alfonso from the fate of the bandit-hero, Salvatore Giuliano. Like Giuliano, Alfonso had been used by the Mafia to mobilise popular resistance against the Fascists. But when the Mafia had changed its tactics after the war and turned against him, she had rescued him from certain death. A strong, clever woman, in short, this character whom Daniela played.

'But I'm not getting this middle period right, Jennie. If only Derek were here to put me through my paces again! It was ridiculous of him to go ahead to set things up in Sicily. They could have sent anyone, that young assistant Sraffa, for example, in his place.'

Jennie shrugged, adding a little darker colour to Daniela's cheek. 'I guess he must have wanted to go.'

'Oh yes, Superman. He thinks he can do everything. Doesn't trust anyone to manage in his place. But he should be here with me,' Daniela moaned, 'I really can't do without him.'

'There, you're ready,' Jennie said matter-of-factly.

Daniela looked at her shrewdly. 'You really don't approve of my carrying on, do you? *Disgrazia*, you're saying to yourself. A spoiled childish woman. I'm right, no?'

Jennie flushed. 'I know it's a difficult part.'

'Difficult! It's impossible. And that director, Matthew, he's, how do you say, useless. Kind, yes, but he understands nothing. I have a good mind to refuse to work without Derek on the set. I shall go and tell him so now.'

Jennie looked at her aghast as she marched towards the door. The others in the room stared in equal disbelief. Daniela had not bothered to keep her voice low.

She reached the door, opened it aggressively, hesitated, took a step out, turned round, looked at her audience and then raised her arms in a dramatic 'what's the use' gesture. She came back to sit in her chair.

'No, I shall be a good girl. I know we're working to a tight schedule and money is short. And you would all hate me, *è vero*?'

Jennie smiled, 'If you can match that last performance, Daniela, there should be no problems.'

Daniela burst into a raucous laugh. 'You are beginning to know me, my secretive little English girl! I shall have to watch you. But that was a much better warm-up than the rehearsal.'

Jennie followed Daniela into the main studio and took her place at the side of the set. Daniela, she noticed, paused to have a word with the assistant director, Piero Sraffa. Her gestures were those of a determined matron who held all the keys to power in her tightly-knit family world. When the cameras began to roll, she performed superbly, better than she had done for days. Even her silences were filled with a resilient strength. There were almost no retakes, and at the end of the afternoon, Matthew Tarn congratulated her warmly.

'Yes, but now I am going to ask you a favour,' Jennie overheard Daniela say to him. 'I would like to have a few hours to go shopping tomorrow, before our travels. Could you shoot the scenes which don't include me?' And,' Daniela fixed him with her luminous eyes, 'I would like to take Jennie with me,' she winked at Jennie as Matthew groaned. 'I will not take no for an answer.'

Matthew succumbed. 'All right, but I want you both back here by two, punctually. We'll probably have to work late to catch up.'

Daniela gave him her most gracious smile and turned to Jennie with a gleeful expression. 'If I hadn't been good today, we would have wasted far more time,' she whispered, 'and a little shopping spree is what I need most in the world. You too must need some things for this imminent journey of ours. It will be warm in Sicily and you cannot only ever wear jeans.'

Not altogether at ease about the way in which Daniela had coerced Matthew, Jennie was however pleased. She had wanted to buy some clothes for the trip and hadn't yet managed to find the time. Daniela's offer was something of a godsend.

Next morning promptly at nine Jennie arrived at the Kensington flat the studio had rented for Daniela. On the first floor of a beautifully-kept eighteenth-century terrace, it was elegantly painted in the faintest shade of pastel grey which blended with plush carpets of deep blue. The furniture in the spacious front room was comfortably contemporary—a large cream-coloured velvet sofa, matching easy chairs, gently unobtrusive lighting in a variety of geometric shapes, and a scattering of low coffee tables. Apart from a finely textured silk hanging, and a large pine-framed mirror, the walls were bare. French windows framed by two giant hanging ferns gracefully looked out on to a row of impeccable gardens.

'It is pleasant here, no?' Daniela poured Jennie a mugful of strong aromatic coffee.

'Lovely.'

'A little bit impersonal, like a page out of, how do you call that magazine, *Homes and Gardens*? But pleasant. Come, I will show you the rest.'

The rest consisted of a wonderfully appointed pine-panelled kitchen, a small study with an old rolltop desk and winged chair, and a large French-windowed bedroom with a satin-draped bed. It was this room which had most of Daniela in it, Jennie noted. She had strewn photographs over the dressing table, tacked more up on a body-length mirror, decked jewellery and trinkets on the night-tables, spread her shawls over the back of a magnificent cane chair.

Daniela poised her china coffee mug amidst the make-up on the dressing table and motioned to Jennie, 'Come, I want to show you something.' She pointed to a photograph of a boy of about five with large luminous eyes in a handsomely serious face. 'My son.'

'Son!' Jennie didn't have time to veil her astonishment.

Daniela chuckled, '*Si*, my son, *il mio bellissimo* Giancarlo. I miss him terribly. No, don't look at me like that. I know I am a bad mother, so much away.' She sighed. 'But he is well taken care of by his grandmama and his father. And now it is school time, so he cannot come to see me. Perhaps when we are in Sicily, he will come down for a weekend.'

Jennie's curiosity about Daniela's family arrangements was aroused, but she didn't have the audacity to question her further. As her eyes skimmed the photographs, she saw a tall man of traditionally Italian good looks—strong jaw, dark eyes, Roman nose—standing next to a small boy who might have been a younger version of Daniela's son. And then a familiar face startled her, sea-blue eyes etched into bronzed brow and jutting cheekbones, and she caught her breath.

Daniela followed the course of her gaze. 'It is a fine photo of Derek, no? I took it myself.'

Jennie thought she detected a look of nostalgia on her

face. 'Yes,' she paused and made her voice disinterested. 'Have you known each other for long?'

'Long enough,' Daniela said meaningfully.

Jennie swallowed and changed the subject. 'And this woman here?'

'Oh, that is my *mamma*. She used to be an actress. It is from her I learned my laugh which seems always to make you jump from your skin. She used to tell me when she took me to the theatre, "Now you must laugh, *fortissimo*, from the stomach, so the actors feel there is an appreciative audience. Then they will act even better." '

Jennie smiled, 'I shall remember that.'

'Come, we had better go now, if we are to have enough time to shop properly.' Daniela threw a rough silk jacket over her shoulders. Its lavender tone exactly matched her trousers and blended delicately with the deeper mauve of her shirt. The contrast with her rich auburn curls was striking.

'You look wonderful,' Jennie said to her.

'Except when you make me up, my little one,' Daniela chuckled. 'But then I work on myself, not like you. This,' she pointed to her body like a piece of merchandise, 'is at least half my career, not the most important half, I keep trying to tell them, but half, nonetheless.' She shrugged. 'And when I go shopping I feel I have to look good before I start or else everything I try is wrong. But today, Jennie, I shall concentrate on you. I cannot bear all this natural beauty going to waste.'

Jennie flushed. 'But I don't like clothes, not much anyway, and—well, I haven't much money.'

Daniela's look was like a pat on the back. 'Don't worry, my Jennie, you don't need much to look well. And don't be afraid. I wouldn't turn you into a clotheshorse. Simplicity, that is what you need.'

The two women walked the short distance to Harrods where Daniela had insisted they go.

'We will concentrate on you first, Jennie. I think you

are probably less well prepared for Sicily than I am,' she smiled wryly.

'What I want above all is a pair of white trousers, some shorts and a bikini. Oh yes, and some sandals.' Jennie felt she couldn't let herself be railroaded into buying more than she needed or could afford.

'Yes, that is sensible.'

As soon as they began looking round, Jennie noticed that Daniela had an eye for price as well as style. 'You are surprised, eh?' she smiled at Jennie. 'We Italians are practical people, and in any case, for a long time I did not have so much money as now.'

Jennie pulled out a pair of white jeans from a rackful and Daniela simultaneously handed her a pair of more fashionable linen trousers.

'Try these on as well, and this,' she passed Jennie a creamy white muslin pirate smock with billowing sleeves and a large square collar that finished in a punging V. 'And come out and parade before me. There's nothing I like better.'

Jennie obeyed dutifully, and instantly fell in love with the loose-fitting smock which went wonderfully well with both pairs of trousers.

Daniela approved, '*Bellissima*! Now a little present from me to dress the whole thing up.' She flung a voluminous maroon-red scarf, embossed with thin silver threads, over Jennie's shoulders and tied it, Jennie wasn't quite sure how, over her right arm. 'Perfect! You look like the *amoretta* of some glorious old Sicilian bandit hero.'

Jennie glanced at her reflection in the long mirror. The deep red of the scarf loosely covering the folds of white made the ivory of her skin glow with a suffused warmth and brought out the darkness of her hair. She smiled at her image.

'Yes, you see, you like it. It is better than jeans.'

Daniela, Jennie noted, seemed to take a childlike pleasure out of dressing her. Now her nimble hands untied the scarf and wound it round Jennie's waist. '*E presto*, with a wave of the magic wand, the bandit's *amoretta* becomes a slender Vogue model!'

Jennie chuckled, 'You're a better saleswoman than I've ever encountered! I shall have the lot.'

'Oh, but we're not finished, my Jennie. I must, I absolutely must see your legs. Do you realise in all these weeks you have never worn a dress?'

Jennie demurred, thinking of the slimness of her bank balance. But Daniela insisted, 'How can I look my best if all the women on this film refuse to compete?' she shook her head tragically. 'If you plead poverty, I shall simply have to make you a present.'

Jennie stiffened.

'No? Well then, you shall have to do it for me, as a favour. Besides, I have found just the things,' Daniela smiled gleefully, and led Jennie towards a rack which seemed to be made out of frothy lace. She pulled out a delicate cotton lace skirt with an intricately scalloped hem and a matching lace top finely frilled at neck and shoulders.

Jennie gasped. The garments were beautiful, but far more than she could afford. Daniela pooh-poohed her doubts. 'How many times a year do you go to Sicily? Your bank manager will be kind on the overdraft. You simply wear the clothes to charm him with. *E tutto va bene*.'

Jennie tried on the skirt and top, looked at herself in disbelief and concluded that Daniela was right. Why not splurge for once? For the first time, she corrected herself. She had worked hard enough for it. She walked out of the fitting room, her head held high.

'*Bella!*' Daniela exclaimed as she examined Jennie with a practised eye. 'Now I shall have to work a little harder.'

Jennie smiled, looking at the older woman's elegance. Daniela had nothing to fear from her. Yet she was pleased

with her transformed self. She had never worn clothes like
this before and would certainly never have dared to buy
them on her own.

'But now it's your turn, Daniela. You haven't bought
anything yet.'

'Yes, but first I will buy a present for Giancarlo and
then I must look around privately. I am a little bit fussy,
you know. So you go and buy those shorts you wanted
and I shall come and parade before you when I am
ready.'

Jennie left her things at the cash desk and wandered
around the counters and racks. Yes, she did like Daniela.
She was kind and generous. Yet there was something
about her that made Jennie suspicious, a kind of world-
liness; almost—she grimaced as the word came to her—a
core of ruthlessness. A chill ran through her as she
suddenly remembered Derek's photograph gazing out at
her from Daniela's mirror. Of course, that was it. It was
her relationship to Derek, her proprietorial air towards
him, which had brought the thought to mind. Daniela,
she imagined, would fight to the bitter end to keep her
man, with a total disregard for scruples of any kind.
And—the insight suddenly crystallised from nowhere—
what Daniela was doing now was manipulating Jennie,
winning her over to make sure that she became more
important to her than any fleeting attraction to Derek.

Jennie shuddered and blotted out all the intrigue the
twosome suggested. She chided herself as she looked
through a range of cotton shorts, picking out a white pair
in her size. She was acting like some narrow-minded little
puritan.

She made herself concentrate on a pile of tee-shirts in a
variety of colours. Burrowing through them, she selected
a white one with thin shoulder straps, and an apple green
with short sleeves. Then she found a simple white bikini
and went to try on the lot. On her way to the dressing
room, she spotted a rack of inexpensive sundresses, and

with a devil-may-care grin to her conscience, she pulled out two, a purple crimped full-skirted Indian cotton with a halter top, and a simple white with straight lines and ribboned shoulder straps. As she tried on the clothes, she felt helpless to reject anything. Her pleasure mixed with guilt at her own extravagance, she walked back, bulky bundle in hand, towards where she had left Daniela. She spied her examining herself carefully from all sides in a three-corner mirror. 'I think I have decided. It is perhaps not for Sicily, but for Rome, it will be perfect.' She pirouetted for Jennie, showing off an outfit made up of a loosely cut cream crêpe-de-chine cardigan with a matching camisole and a full black skirt trimmed with broderie anglaise.

'It's lovely,' said Jennie, thinking how odd it was that this low-key classical outfit brought out Daniela's dramatic beauty all the more.

'And there is this,' Daniela showed her a pair of white linen trousers and a voile shirt with large floppy ruffles, 'but I will not try it on for you, since we must now hurry if we are to get some shoes and some lunch.'

The two women paid for the clothes and then took the lift to the shoe department. Jennie hastily selected a pair of white espadrilles which tied round the ankle and, at Daniela's urging, a pair of high-heeled black ankle-strapped sandals. 'To show off those legs we never see,' Daniella chuckled sardonically. 'If we're not careful we shall lose you to some ardent Mafioso chief. But before that we must eat. The food in Sicily, as I remember it, is dreadful, so I shall treat you to some proper Italian food now. Don't laugh at me, my Jennie, we Romans are particular about what we put into our stomachs.'

Daniela led her through back streets to what seemed from the pavement an unpretentious *trattoria*. The white-shirted waiter welcomed her by name and ushered them to a back room where green-chequered tablecloths covered large and small tables, most of them filled with

men in business suits. Small bunches of brightly yellow
daffodils graced the tables, giving the room a jolly air.

'Now is my chance to fatten you up a little,' said
Daniela playfully as she looked at the menu. 'You must
let me order for you. First a *pasta*—*tortelloni alla crema*, you
rarely get that here in London; and then some *scallopini*,
yes?'

Jennie nodded.

'And a little white wine to celebrate our successful
shopping, *si*? With some *aqua minerale* to sober us up for
work. Good.' Daniela ordered quickly in Italian and the
food arrived almost instantly. Jennie tucked into her
tortelloni with gusto. The small spinach-filled morsels in a
delicate cream sauce were delicious.

Daniela watched her. 'I was right? It is good, isn't it?'
Jennie smiled her appreciation. Daniela, she noticed, was
only picking at her melon.

'Isn't yours good?' she queried.

Daniela grimaced, 'Unlike you, my Jennie, I must
watch my figure. These curves, they must not grow too
large.'

Jennie protested, but the actress cut her off. Taking a
sip of her wine, she turned the full glow of her grey-green
eyes on Jennie and asked abruptly, 'Tell me, Jennie, have
you any men friends?'

Jennie felt the *pasta* in her mouth turning to a gluey
mass as she tried to swallow. She focussed her eyes on her
plate away from Daniela's scrutiny. 'Not at the moment,'
she managed casually enough.

Daniela's scrutiny continued, 'But you have had friends,
I mean lovers, in the past. *Si*?'

Jennie began to feel indignant. Daniela had no right to
intrude herself in this way. She raised her eyes from her
plate and looked at the actress coolly. 'That is surely none
of your concern.'

The edge of formality in Jennie's voice made Daniela
smile, 'No, you are right, that is none of my concern.' She

placed a piece of melon in her mouth reflectively. 'Perhaps a sad love affair. You do not wish to speak of it?'

Jennie shrugged and forced herself to swallow what was now tasteless food.

'Yes, I understand, it is painful.'

The two women ate in silence for a short time. Then when the waiter came to clear their plates, Daniela caught Jennie's eye and held it.

'You know, I think Derek is interested in you.'

Jennie felt the blood draining from her face. So that was what Daniela had been leading up to! She wouldn't give her the satisfaction of knowledge.

'In me?' Jennie asked, looking startled. She put on her most ingenuous air.

Daniela chuckled, 'You mean you haven't noticed?'

Jennie gazed at her with wide-eyed innocence, secretly surprised at the acting talents which had suddenly surfaced in her.

As the waiter served them with two plates of lemon-scented veal, Daniela laughed outright.

'Derek would be mortified if he suspected you hadn't noticed!'

Jennie dug into her veal and *zucchini* with new-found relish. 'This is delicious,' she offered.

'Yes, the food here is very good,' Daniela replied, but she was not altogether ready to drop the subject of Derek. 'Tell me, Jennie, how is it that Derek knew about your painting and I did not?'

A variety of half-lies suggested themselves to Jennie, but she decided on a non-committal shrug. 'Perhaps someone in the studio mentioned it to him.'

'Yes, perhaps,' Daniela reflected. 'Yes, he is so curious, he always seems to find out everything.'

Jennie thought the subject had now been put to rest, but after a few moments Daniela began again.

'You know, Jennie, Derek is a powerful man—a most powerful man. And if, as I suspect, he is interested in you,

you will notice it sooner or later, and then *presto*,' she snapped her fingers dramatically, 'if you are not strong, he will take you over. But not for long, no. He will grow tired, grow interested in someone else. And you will suffer, *mamma mia*, you will suffer. But worse, because he is so powerful, you will find you are unfit for other men.' Daniela shook her head sadly, and then looked up, bright-eyed, a tremulous smile on her lips. '*Basta*. I am taking this little scenario a little too far. Let us talk of other things.'

She pushed her plate away a little and reaching for her bag took out a packet of cigarettes. She offered one to Jennie, who accepted. Smoking was not something she did often, but now she felt a cigarette between her fingers would give her strength to face any other conversational surprises Daniela might have in store.

Daniela lit their cigarettes with a slender gold lighter and took a long puff. 'Some coffee, my Jennie. Oh no, first a sweet for you, a flan or some *cassata*.'

Jennie demurred, 'Coffee is all I want. A *capuccino*, if they have one.'

Daniela signalled to the waiter and then looked closely at Jennie again. 'I hope you are not angry with me, Jennie. You know, I always speak my mind. Perhaps a little too cearly.'

Jennie avoided her eyes, but shook her head.

'I would like us to be friends, but you must learn to live with my impetuous mouth.' Daniela chuckled, her good humour seemingly restored. 'Now, you know who would be a fine match for you? Piero Sraffa. So handsome, with those wonderful black slanting eyes, and also, I discovered today, far from stupid. Even intelligent.'

Jennie felt herself prickle. 'You should know, Daniela, that I'm perfectly happy without a man in my life. I have far too much to fill it as it is. I'm not so interested in them as you seem to be.'

'Bravo, Jennie! You are right to be angry. I am an

interfering woman,' she smiled wryly, 'like my own *mamma*. And it is my fate. I need men, so I imagine every woman does.' She grimaced as if examining her own foibles, and then laughed richly, 'I am a fool. But come, we must get back to work or that Matthew will be angry with me too. We will take a taxi.'

As Daniela paid the bill and instructed the waiter to order a taxi for them, Jennie examined her discreetly. She didn't know what to make of Daniela—on the one hand, she resented her insinuations, her interference, and fundamentally disliked her sudden flares of temper; on the other, she was drawn by her warm generosity. She pushed her suspicions out of her mind. After all, whatever her motives, Daniela was worldly-wise enough to be right about Derek, that was certain. Jennie shrugged and put all thought of him well out of reach.

The two women bundled their parcels into the taxi which awaited them at the kerb and relaxed into the seats.

'Much as I love your London taxis, my Jennie, I shall be supremely happy to be back in Italy. And the Sicilian sun . . . it will be marvellous!'

Jennie echoed Daniela's enthusiasm and as the car pulled up at the studios, she thanked her profusely for the shopping expedition, the lovely present, the lunch, everything.

'I enjoyed it too,' Daniela assured her. 'And it is my way of thanking you for all the hard work you have done on me. And now you must do some more. Poor Jennie, and I shall grow angry as I turn into an old hag under your skilful hands.'

Jennie laughed as the taxi driver gave Daniela an enraptured look. Some old hag!

CHAPTER FIVE

JENNIE clenched her teeth and tried to pretend her stomach hadn't suddenly plunged down to her knees as the plane made its way through turbulent skies over northern Italy. Piero Sraffa gave her a sympathetic smile and handed her a cigarette.

'It should help,' he said, lighting her cigarette and taking a deep puff of his own.

Jennie noticed the elegance of his long slender hands and wondered again whether Daniela had been instrumental in seating them together. When she had boarded the plane earlier that morning, she had found Piero in the window seat next to hers. Hearing that it was her first time aboard a plane, he had gallantly offered her his place, and she had accepted, eager to see the sights from this unknown height. A little after take-off Daniela had come wandering out of the first class compartment at the front of the plane, said hello, and given Jennie a quick covert wink before sauntering off.

Jennie shrugged off the thought of any possible manipulation and returned her attention to Piero. Whatever the case, he had proved an excellent companion, assuaging her visible fear of the plane's motion with humorous anecdotes, plying her with drink so that she was now quite lightheaded. His careful English was word-perfect, even in intonation—quite unlike Daniela's occasional rhythmic flights.

Jennie smiled in delight as the dense cloud beneath them cleared to exhibit the snow-capped Alps.

'Better?' Piero's mellow baritone intruded on her thoughts.

She nodded and took a last long sip of her gin and tonic.

'Shall I get you another?'

'No,' Jennie found herself giggling. 'By the time we land, I won't be able to walk in a straight line!'

'No one here will be in a state to notice,' he laughed, gesturing towards the empty glasses on all the trays in seeing distance. He buzzed for the stewardess and ordered another round of drinks. 'In any case, you can sleep it off this afternoon. I should think everyone will be tumbling into bed for a siesta.'

'What luxury!' Jennie breathed. She suddenly felt elated, as if each successive mile that separated her from England lifted another anxiety from her shoulders. 'It's too good to be true—planes, hotels,' she let her eyes rove over Piero's face, 'handsome men, siestas.' She crossed one long white-clad leg over another and looked at him with just a hint of flirtation in her smile.

His dark heavily-lashed eyes flashed merrily at her. 'You sound like a little girl setting off for her first and most wonderful adventure!'

Jennie chuckled, 'If I'm honest with myself, that's exactly how I feel.'

'Well, you shall have to let me help you make it special. There's no doubt that Sicily is an adventure, but whether it's always wonderful . . .' His handsome face suddenly looked concerned. 'You know, when Sicily became part of Italy, the Sicilians had a rather bitter joke about it. They said the Italian boot was giving the island an almighty kick, and I'm afraid they were right. We northerners had no idea then, and it's not all that much better now, of the conditions people on the island lived in. We imposed taxes on tiny peasant holdings which produced barely enough for families to live on. The Sicilians rose up against us, and in 1866 we sent forty thousand troops to quell a rebellion.' He shook his head sadly. 'And all the subsequent misunderstanding only helped to kindle separatist feelings and entrench the Mafia. You'll see, they don't like us . . . and with justification. They're fiercely independent. But I'm being lugubrious,' he flashed a startlingly white smile at her. 'And you want a wonderful Sicilian adventure.'

'Oh no, do please go on. I'm so amazingly ignorant.'

He looked at her seriously for a moment and then shook his head. 'No, now you must look out of the window or you'll miss the sight of the boot kicking Sicily,' Piero chuckled, his eyes warm as they took in her face.

Jennie turned away from him and stared out of the window. She could feel his eyes still on her, but somehow they didn't make her uncomfortable. She decided she liked Piero. There was a straightforwardness about him, a naturalness which she hadn't expected in a man of such elegant good looks and such evident sophistication. She smiled to herself. The world was full of surprises today, not least that of the astounding landscape beneath her.

The blue sea looked motionless from this height, and as the plane descended, toy-like slopes and white play houses seemed to rise out of a midday haze. Then something made Jennie catch her breath and she tugged at Piero's sleeve. He edged his head in beside hers to look out the window. There, slightly to one side of the plane, a small puff of dark smoke emerged out of a charred crater—a black pit in the belly of which something obscure boiled and rumbled.

'Etna,' Piero told her, and then added mysteriously, 'Vulcan's forge: when he walks, the earth trembles; when he coughs, volcanoes erupt. Abode too of Vulcan's one-eyed helpers, the hideous Cyclops. So beware,' Piero teased, 'if you meet any ill-mannered giants on this island. They're wont to devour strange young ladies!'

Jennie was too rapt by the sight to respond. Around the central crater, she noticed there were hundreds of smaller holes in the earth's crust, all of which seemed to be alive, bubbling away. She shivered. There was

something menacing in the atmosphere, the walls of black
lava blocks which she could now see, the black terraced
soil. As the plane moved away from Etna to reveal pasture
land and then lush vineyards and orchards, Jennie
breathed a sigh of relief. Then she bent to take her pad
out of her large bag and made a hasty sketch of what the
crater and its smaller sisters had looked like from the sky.
As she finished, she grew aware of Piero's nearness, his
eyes on her pad. She drew away.

He looked at her from the deep recesses of his eyes.
'I'm sorry if I disturbed you. It's a good sketch.'

She thanked him, aware of his sincerity, and then as
the stewardess's voice came over the speaker announcing
their landing, she tucked the pad back into her bag and
clenched the arms of her seat tightly.

'It will all be over quickly,' Piero murmured gently,
noticing her fear. 'Just keep swallowing.'

Jennie felt her stomach lurch, saw the ground coming
towards her, felt a bump and then heard what seemed to
be engines revving loudly.

'He's braking,' Piero explained. 'We're here.'

Jennie felt a thrill pass through her as they emerged
from the plane into the clear noon sunlight. As warm air
enveloped her, she was grateful for her white trousers,
grateful too for the sunglasses she had purchased at the
airport at the last minute. She followed Piero through the
formalities of Immigration and into the baggage room
crowded with people all of whom seemed to be licking
ice-cream. The room exploded with noise, but the sounds
she could make out were quite unlike Italian, full of low
guttural inflections.

'Sicilians are amazing,' Piero exclaimed. 'Whole
families will travel for miles to see a relative off or welcome
someone. And the dialect!' He groaned. 'I'm lucky if I
can make it out.'

He took her bag for her and they walked out to the
arrival hall where they were to meet the others before

boarding a bus which would take them to their hotel. Lounging casually by a newspaper kiosk, Jennie noticed a tall lithe form. She turned her eyes away hurriedly, but it was too late. Derek was walking towards them, his long muscular legs encased in gleaming white trousers, his bare brown arms swinging loosely at his side. 'Hello, Piero,' he shook his hand. 'Hello, Jennie.'

She raised her eyes to meet his and was momentarily shocked by their forgotten blueness, even deeper now that his skin and hair had taken on an added bronze glow. He held her eyes for a moment, then bent to kiss her lightly on the cheek. As he moved away, he whispered lightly, out of Piero's hearing, 'Done any good nudes lately?' His tone was sardonic and she felt herself flush.

'Only as many as could fill a week,' she muttered beneath her breath.

He darted a glance at her, but before he could say anything Daniela was upon them with Matthew in tow. She embraced Derek warmly, kissing him on both cheeks. Then she wound her arm through his. 'Well, shall we go? I hope you've brought a car for us. I don't think I could face a beastly Sicilian bus.'

Derek laughed, 'Anything for *la signora* Colombi and Signor Tarn. There's room for you two as well,' he said, turning to Jennie and Piero, 'I thought Daniela might have brought a lot more luggage than I can see.'

'I have learned to travel light now,' Daniela retorted, looking dramatically insulted, 'but do join us.'

Watching her, Jennie suddenly took hold of Piero's arm and Daniela threw her a wicked smile. 'Come, my children. Derek will drive us through the wonders of Sicily.'

Derek led them towards a large silver open-top Fiat parked randomly in front of the airport building. They piled into the car, Daniela in front with Derek, muttering that she was undoubtedly taking her life in her hands now that she was on an Italian road again; the three of them tucked closely together in the back seat, a suitcase balanced on their laps.

Jennie could feel her excitement mounting by the second as Derek drove the car swiftly, smoothly, over the motorway, its lanes divided by the lush pinks and reds of an oleander hedge. Everything—stones, trees, houses, even the traffic they encountered after they had skirted Palermo and found themselves in an industrial suburb— seemed to be etched in a crystal clarity Jennie had never before experienced. She felt as if her eyes, her senses were alive for the first time. When the car wound its way along a road banked by lemon groves, she let out an audible gasp.

'Are you all right?' Piero looked at her in concern.

She nodded. 'It's just—oh, all this beauty. I know it sounds ridiculous, but it's as if a film had lifted from my eyes.'

He squeezed her arm, then chuckled. 'That film is what we Italians so love about England-mist, we call it. It smooths the edges of Mediterranean hardness.'

Jennie suddenly caught Derek's glance in the rear view mirror. He seemed to be glaring at her and automatically she moved away from Piero, then stopped herself. She wouldn't let Derek make her uncomfortable now. Her gaze moved again over the citrus groves and all at once encountered what she had quite unconsciously been look- ing for: a glistening expanse of blue stretching into the horizon—the sea. Another gasp involuntarily escaped her.

Piero laughed, 'If you keep this up. I won't want to see anything with anyone but you! It makes me happy just to take in your pleasure.'

Jennie smiled, pushing fingers through her windswept hair. 'I think it must be all the drink you plied me with on the plane.'

He gave her a warm look. 'We're almost there. The hotel we're all booked into is just outside Cefalu. After lunch and the necessary siestas, I'll show you round. Quite selfishly—so that I can watch your face,' he added, chuckling.

The car pulled up in front of a large modern hotel tucked between hills and overlooking the sea. Matthew was first out and gallantly lifted the case off Jennie's lap before opening the door for Daniela. A dark, quick-eyed porter came and helped them with their bags. At reception, they gave their names and were handed keys by a comfortable-looking woman of middle years.

'You're just a few doors away from me,' Jennie heard Derek say softly at her side. 'Perhaps you'll come and visit.'

She flushed at his tone and turned away, quite unsure of the direction.

'The lift's to your right,' Derek called after her, a taunting edge in his voice.

Piero came up behind her and pointed the direction. 'Would you like to have some lunch after you've unpacked?'

Jennie nodded gratefully, 'I won't be long.'

The room, Jennie noted as she opened the door on to dimness, was comfortable but unspectacular: two single beds, separated by a night table, a large chest of drawers, a mirrored wardrobe, a door opening on to a spacious tiled bathroom. A low knock stopped her inspection and she turned to find the porter with her case. He deposited it on a rack and then moved to draw the curtains slightly. Jennie gasped: there in all its tantalising blueness was the sea. She slid open the glass door and stepped on to a terrace which stretched the width of the room and fed her eyes on the sight. Minutes slipped by before she remembered that she was meant to be meeting Piero for lunch. She unpacked quickly and pulled on her new white sun-frock, washed her face and tried to brush some order into her windswept hair. Then, not worrying too much about her reflected image, she went downstairs to find the dining room.

It was a semi-circular room, its light muted by shutters, but she spied Piero waiting for her at the far end. He had gravitated towards one of the few tables which looked on to an expanse of blue.

'I thought you'd prefer this to shadier corners, despite the heat.'

She smiled her thanks and looked around. She could see Derek at a table across the room, deep in conversation with Matthew. Piero followed her gaze. 'I should really be with them to catch up on what Derek's managed so far, but I thought I'd enjoy your company briefly first. I stress your company, because the food is bound to be dreadful.'

As if on cue, a waiter arrived with two plates of steaming risotto.

'But it looks good,' Jennie exclaimed.

'On the first day, perhaps,' Piero grimaced, 'but after a week of it in this weather—well, you'll see.'

Jennie sipped her wine slowly and heaped large forkfuls of the oddly comforting rice into her mouth. She could feel Piero's eyes on her as she gazed out at the sea's inviting blue, but somehow they didn't discomfit her. She looked at him languorously and gave him a warm smile. He returned it.

'I can see that you have all the makings of a mermaid,' he chuckled. 'You look at that sea with such longing. If that gaze were turned on me, I would find it irresistible.' He passed a finger down her cheek, tracing its curve, while his eyes held hers. Jennie looked unafraid into their depths, losing herself there for a moment.

'I hate to break up this amorous duet, Piero,' a deep voice at her side intruded, 'but Matthew and I would like to have a word with you—if Miss Lewis can bear to let you go, that is,' Derek added with an abrasive irony.

Jennie felt a flush creeping over her face. But Piero's voice was cool as he replied, 'I'll be over in a minute.'

Derek left them, a hard glint in his eye as he nodded to Jennie.

'Sorry to have to abandon you before coffee, Miss Lewis,' Piero imitated Derek's tone and then laughed. 'Perhaps I can make up for it by taking you into Cefalu for dinner this evening?'

Jennie nodded her acceptance and returned her eyes to the sea. Yes, it was what she most wanted now, the feel of that water on her skin. She left her table, kept her eyes well away from where the men were sitting, and went to her room. There she discovered that Kathy Walsh, the wardrobe mistress, had now settled in and was comfortably stretched out on the terrace.

'This is heaven, Jennie. Slip into something skimpy and join me,' Kathy called out to her.

Jennie walked out into the terrace's bright light. 'I think I'll take a stroll down to the beach first. I can't wait to get into that water.'

'Suit yourself. I wanted a bit of a tan before exposing myself to other eyes.' Kathy looked down at her white flesh disparagingly. 'This bright sun makes all this pallor look ghastly.'

Jennie shrugged. 'Everyone will be napping now in any case.' She slipped a bikini on under her sun-dress, put a towel and her sketchpad into a canvas bag, and went down to reception to ask the way to the beach. She was directed towards a narrow pebbly path which seemed to have been hewn out of the grey-black rock bordering it on both sides. Almost like a tunnel, Jennie thought, except for the blue sky overhead. She followed the steep incline, meeting no one on the way, and after a few minutes found herself face to face with the dazzling turquoise of the sea.

The beach was a small sandy cove sheltered from all eyes by towering boulders which dipped into the waves. A mid-afternoon sun played on the water, the rocks, the sand. Jennie threw off her sandals and let her toes taste the warmth. Then she stretched luxuriantly out on the sand, propping her head up on her bag and gazing out at the sea through half-closed lids. Still fiercely bright, the sun baked her body, burning out any tautness, making her mind blankly indolent. Images floated randomly past, none carrying more weight than another. Only the warmth of the sand beneath her and the blazing heat above seemed to have any reality. Her fingers roamed sensuously over the sand's surface, smoothing its texture. She lay there blissfully remote from past or future, simply soaking up the sensations of the moment, the rhythmic lapping of waves on stone.

Only when she felt the sun had penetrated her very bones did she rise and in a kind of lazy stupor make her way towards the water. The coolness of the waves played round her ankles, and after a momentary hesitation, she plunged her hot body into the water, swimming with strong regular strokes beyond the boulders into the open sea. To catch her breath, she turned over on her back and gazed towards the shoreline. From this distance she could see over the cove up the incline to the hotel and beyond it, to the purple outline of the mountains. To her left, clearly visible, was the little fishing town of Cefalu and other small coves. She closed her eyes, relaxing on the gentle waves, letting the sea carry her where it would.

Suddenly she felt a tug at the bottom part of her bikini and the sound of aggressive laughter. Her eyes bolted open and she began to tread water frantically. On either side of her were two taunting, coarse-featured youths. She couldn't understand what they were saying, but the sense of their words was clear to her. Jennie began to swim towards the distant shore, but their rapid strokes brought them to her side and, laughing loudly, they grabbed at her legs and arms until her panic mounted into a scream. She thrashed about wildly in the water and at one moment felt it submerge her. An image of the giant one-eyed Cyclops which Piero had laughingly described darted across her mind, and gasping for breath, she forced her head above the waves. One of the youths lunged at her, encircling her waist with his arm. Jennie felt a scream rising to her throat again, but it was strangled by a wave.

Then as her mind focussed once more, she made out a new voice, resonant with authority, felt the arm leave her waist and as her head dipped again beneath the waves, a new pair of arms pulling her upward and firmly guiding her towards the shore.

Without knowing quite how she had arrived there, she felt sand warming the length of her frame, strong hands rubbing sense back into her body; heard a voice enquiring gently, 'Are you all right?'

She turned over, too breathless to speak. Derek was kneeling beside her, his eyes filled with concern. He was massaging her arms, her wrists, her legs, her ankles, and as the warm sensation removed the panic from her veins, she found her voice.

'Thanks for helping,' she said softly, lifting herself up on her elbows and then sinking back on the sand as her head filled with dizziness.

He stretched out beside her and looked at her sternly. 'Whatever made you swim out so far alone?' he asked gruffly.

She shrugged, her eyes filling with tears.

He placed his arm around her waist and rubbed her gently. 'Never mind, you'll be all right in a few minutes. Just breathe deeply.'

Jennie did as she was told, surprised at her own lack of resistance, but too weak to move or to demur. She closed her eyes to the sun and then as she grew aware of the strokes becoming a caress, she raised herself slowly, loath to break the quiet rhythm, but sensing a new danger.

'I think I'm all right now. I'd better go back to my room.'

'Are you quite sure you can walk?' Derek looked at her sceptically.

She nodded, rising unsteadily to her feet. Derek put out an arm to help her and then as her legs trembled visibly, wound it round her, giving her the support of his hard body. She leaned against him heavily for a moment and then drew away, steeling herself to walk free of him. His eyes had a gleam of irony in them as they met hers. 'I won't bite, you know, or do anything uncouth.'

Jennie could find nothing to say in reply, but as she took in the full hard length of him as he stood before her, long muscular legs planted firmly in the sand, golden chest bare above black swimming trunks, tousled hair wetly gleaming in the sun, she could feel a magnetic charge drawing her towards him. She turned away abruptly, pulling her sundress over her shoulders, happy to be able to hide her face from him momentarily. As she emerged again, he was beside her, running a large hand through the tangled wetness of her hair. She shuddered.

'Come on,' Derek picked up her bag and put his arm around her shoulder. 'And stop playing games with me now, or we'll lose you before the filming even starts!'

Jennie flushed, but let him guide her up the narrow path, grateful, if she dared admit it to herself, for his steadying presence.

He led her to his room without giving her a chance to protest, sat her down in a comfortable armchair, and turning his back ordered her to take off her wet bikini. She obeyed, slipping it out from under her dress. As she huddled back into the chair, shivering a little, he threw her a large towelling robe. She snuggled into its dryness and curled up in the large chair.

He looked at her and shook his head. 'Didn't your mother warn you about Sicilian men?'

Without knowing quite why, Jennie found herself laughing stridently. 'She didn't have much chance to warn me of anything,' she said, and found all at once that the laughter had turned to sobs. They came fast and convulsive and were still shaking her as Derek handed her a large glass of brandy and ordered her to drink up. The burning sensation from throat to stomach brought her back to herself. She wiped her tears with the robe's floppy sleeve and looked up to meet Derek's eyes. He seemed to be watching her closely and she stiffened with embarrassment.

'I'm sorry about all that. I must be a little hysterical,' she said in a low voice.

'Silly woman! What is there to be sorry about? It would be unnatural if you didn't cry from the sheer shock of it all.'

He looked at her questioningly. 'Why didn't your mother have a chance to warn you?' he asked.

Jennie swallowed a returning sob.

'She died when I was seven.'

'I'm sorry,' he offered gently, reaching for her hand which she quickly pulled away. 'And your father didn't make any paternal gestures of advice?' he queried after a moment.

Jennie looked beyond him, towards the blue which crept through the shutters. 'He died before her, in an accident,' she said flatly, a note of hardness entering her tone.

'I see,' Derek breathed reflectively. 'So that accounts for a little of your remoteness, your insistent self-reliance.'

Jennie shrugged.

'Who brought you up, then?' His eyes were hard on her, urging her to meet his.

'Relations. An aunt and uncle,' she said tersely, and rose to her feet gesturing an end to the session.

'Sit down, Jennie,' he ordered her with a firmness which harboured no defiance. Then, his voice gentle, he added, 'You're in no shape to go anywhere yet.'

Jennie sank back into the chair and closed her eyes. The room started to whirl round her and she opened them again quickly, only to find Derek's gaze fixed on her.

'You're a very beautiful woman, you know, when you relax your mouth a little.'

She threw him a scathing look. 'I hardly need your

compliments at the moment.'

He chuckled. 'I'm sure that's right. I shall have to plan them to meet demand. Do you think there might be a time when that demand is made?' The mocking tilt returned to his lips. 'Or have you given up our sex for ever, oh, mysterious lady?'

Jennie flushed and turned her head away from him.

'Why do you avoid men, Jennie?' he asked, his voice suddenly soft. 'Did one of us behave badly towards you, hurt you? Was your uncle unkind to you?'

She glared at him, hating him for his questioning, for the way he was groping near the truth; wanting to hurt him for tampering with her composure, infringing on that private self she so carefully shielded.

'I simply don't like them, any of them,' she said defiantly, and lurched out of her chair.

Derek followed her movements with a wicked light in his eye, and then springing lithely to his feet, put a stopping hand on her shoulder. 'Funny, I sometimes get a distinctly different impression. It's when you look at me with a particular light in your eye.'

She gazed up at him now for a long moment. Words had left her and she was intensely aware of his hand on her shoulder, suddenly aware too that the broad expanse of his chest was still bare, of the golden smoothness of the skin stretching tautly over shoulders, the muscled trunk of neck holding up the head with perfect symmetry.

Derek's laugh broke the silence. 'There you go. You look as if you're just about ready to start on that nude study again. It's not a look that testifies to a dislike of men . . .'

The blood came rushing into Jennie's face. She turned her glance from him and bolted from under his hand. 'I think I'd better get back to my room now. Thanks for saving my life,' she added, managing to put an element of politeness into her tone.

'I don't know about your life, but certainly your

honour. I think you'll just have to leave it in my care while you're here. No more solitary escapades without my specific permission. Is that agreed?'

There was a seriousness beneath the banter in his tone and in his eyes as Jennie met their gaze.

She shrugged. 'It was just that first burst of sun, the sheer delight of the sea . . .' She closed her eyes for a second, remembering the bliss of it all. 'I think it must have stunned me, but I'll be on my guard now.'

She took off his robe and handed it to him. Her dress, still moist from her bathing suit, clung a little transparently to her skin, moulding her slender curves. Derek's eyes roved over her body and as he took the robe from her, he pulled her towards him, wrapping her in his arms. 'As long as it's not against me,' he whispered in her ear. 'I want to test this supposed dislike of men for myself.'

Before she could move away, his lips sought hers hungrily, forcing her mouth open with a searching intensity. His large hands roaming over the small of her back kept her pinned to him and as she felt the tautness of his firm body against hers, strange new sensations enveloped her. Little licks of flame leapt up her thighs, making her pulse beat heavily. Taking on a life of their own, her hands tasted the tight satin of his skin, finding their way along his back, his chest. His kiss deepened and she felt her limbs swaying powerless, turning molten. He pressed her more tightly against him and with one sure step lifted her on to the bed. She could smell the sea on him, taste the salt on his lips. Her mouth opened to his with its own hunger. A low moan escaped him and his hand cupped the shape of one firm breast, delicately tracing the outline of a nipple.

'Are you sure, you don't like us, Jennie? Quite sure?' he whispered huskily, stifling any response she could make with a kiss which seemed to reach every part of her body. Then, through the thudding in her temples, Jennie distinguished a remote voice, not her own, calling, 'Derek!' and a knocking. He jumped up with a mumbled 'damn' just as the door opened to reveal Daniela's shape in the muted light of the room.

Jennie closed her eyes, unable to move, unwilling to have to confront anyone, wishing somehow that the moment would vanish like a bad dream. She lay quite still. She could hear Derek whispering, 'Ssh!' and then in low tones saying, 'It's Jennie, she's asleep. She had a rather nasty turn at the beach and I made her come back here.'

Jennie opened her eyes and sat up on the bed. She felt oddly cold, irritated at Derek's half truths, at the way he was obviously placating Daniela. 'You can stop whispering, I'm awake,' she said loudly. 'Hello, Daniela, has Derek been filling you in on my Sicilian adventure?'

Daniela eyed her suspiciously, taking in the crumpled bedclothes, the flush on Jennie's cheeks, and she looked slowly from her to Derek and back again.

'Tell me about this Sicilian adventure,' she said to Jennie, moving to sit at the edge of the bed, smoothing out the bedspread with exaggerated gestures.

'I think Jennie's in no state to chat,' Derek intervened, his voice calm.

'Too true,' Jennie replied, a hint of malice in her tone. 'And I'm sure Derek can tell you about it far better than I can. He did a wonderful job of defending my honour.' She got off the bed, anger now making her movements steady. 'And miraculously, it's still intact,' she threw Derek a contemptuous look.

'It was pure luck that I came along . . . and that I can swim.' His voice was politely cool, but Jennie read an anger in his eyes that matched hers.

'I was born lucky,' Jennie flaunted back irrelevantly. 'Well, I'll leave you two now.' She reached for her canvas bag, sensing Daniela's eyes on her back. Then she turned to face her and offered casually, in a semi-whisper, but quite loud enough for Derek to hear, 'I'm off to dinner with Piero tonight and I want some time to make myself fetching.'

Daniela smiled, the suspicion leaving her eyes. 'Have a lovely evening with him,' she said, emphasising each word for Derek's benefit and giving Jennie a large wink.

Jennie turned to Derek. 'Thanks. For everything,' she added tauntingly.

He opened the door for her, 'Any time, Jennie. Any time.' His voice beneath its controlled coolness bore a distinct challenge.

Jennie went back to her room and flung herself down on her bed. Her heart was racing, inchoate thoughts pounding through her head. She took a deep breath to calm herself, but it served only to release the tears. They streamed down her face on to her pillow and she wasn't too sure whether she was crying because of the panic brought on by the youths' assault or because of Derek and his evident preference of Daniela over her. She should, she chided herself mentally, feel exhilarated. Touching Derek, being touched by him, was so unlike anything she had experienced before, so different from Max. That shuddering repulsion that she had felt, that sense of her skin crawling, had been replaced by . . . She moaned softly and shut her eyes tight, forbidding her body to live the memory, the exquisite delight of Derek's skin on hers. It was as if she had been jolted into sensuality. She licked a salty tear from her lip. The sea. It was the sea that had done it. The taste of the sea on Derek's mouth.

CHAPTER SIX

THE sound of a door closing startled Jennie frnm 1 light sleep.

'Oh, I'm sorry, Jen,' said Kathy. 'Did I wake you? I just came back to get dressed for dinner. God, that setting sun out there is heavenly!'

Jennie wiped the sleep from her eyes and moved to open the shutters on to the terrace. A bright globe within hand reach suffused the sea, the room, everything with a rosy golden light. She gazed out at the spectacle and breathed in the salt-scented air. After all, it was good to be alive. She glanced at her watch and noticed the lateness of the hour.

'I'd better start getting dressed too. Do you want a shower first, Kathy?'

Kathy shook her mop of straw-coloured curls. 'Had one while you were out. It is super here, isn't it? I even dared a dip in the pool—lovely!'

'So was the sea,' said Jennie, deliberately avoiding all mention of her misadventure. Best really to wipe that from her mind.

'And you're beginning to tan.' Kathy flicked on a light to examine Jennie by. 'Lucky you! Not all this freckly pinkness,' she looked at herself disparagingly in the mirror. 'Still, on with some clothes.'

Jennie took her robe into the bathroom with its pretty ochre and white tiles, stripped herself bare and gazed at her reflection. Yes, she was beginning to tan: the bikini marks and the flushed glow of her face made that clear. She turned on the shower and stepped into the steady stream, soaping her hair and body thoroughly, feeling the

salt prickle her skin where it had been made sensitive by
the sun. Then she towelled herself gently dry and rubbed
baby lotion all over herself. The touch of her hand on her
skin brought back the memory of Derek's bolder caress. A
wave of anger flooded over her. How dared he make her
feel like some wanton second-rate hussy who would
comply in keeping their dealings secret before the estab-
lished partner, the wife, Daniela? And she wasn't his wife
to boot. Rage swept over her and she pulled on her new
clothes with unwonted ferocity. She had a good mind to
tell Daniela about her cherished Derek. It would serve
them both right. But she knew she wouldn't. And in any
case, something told her that Daniela already knew.

Jennie looked at herself in the ruffled pirate smock
Daniela had chosen for her. It did suit her wonderfully
well, and with the new colour in her cheeks, she looked
quite at her best. She brushed her hair gleaming dry and,
to celebrate Sicily, made up her eyes with tints of mauve
and grey, and put on some pale lipstick.

Kathy looked her over. 'Smashing! You look quite a
new woman. The Mediterranean suits you.'

'And you,' said Jennie, taking in Kathy's brightly-
coloured print which would have looked garish in
England, the blue of her eyes over the jolly freckles on her
small nose. 'Perhaps you'll let me do a drawing of you
tomorrow.'

'Oh, would you, Jen? I can't wait!' She put her arm
through Jennie's. 'Let's pretend we're two Italian women
and flounce down to the bar together.'

'Just let me get my new scarf. It may turn cool later.'
Jennie draped the yards of bright fabric over her shoulders
in loose imitation of what Daniela had done and the two
girls left the room.

The whole crew seemed already to be assembled in the
bar, and Kathy and Jennie's arrival was greeted with
playful wolf whistles and calls from all corners, 'Over here,
signorine!' A quick glance round the room reassured Jennie

that neither Derek nor Daniela were there, but in a far corner she could see Piero sitting with Matthew Tarn at a small table. She made her way towards them, greeting others on the way. Piero stood up politely as she approached. His satin-dark eyes were warm with approval.

'The siesta has done you obvious good,' he said, beckoning her to sit in the armchair next to him. 'You look quite radiant.'

Jennie smiled a little remotely and sat down. 'I hope you've had a chance to rest too.'

'Rest?' Matthew intervened. 'I've had him running about all afternoon.' He laughed. 'But I'll leave him in your hands now, Jennie. You can soothe away his weariness.' He smiled at them both. 'Have a good evening.'

'A drink, Jennie? Campari and soda, perhaps? It's nice in the heat and then we can stroll down to Cefalu for dinner. It's not too far to walk.'

'Sounds wonderful. I'm only sorry it will be too dark to do some sightseeing. I remember reading that Cefalu has a beautiful old cathedral.'

Piero chuckled. 'You've been doing your homework too well. If there's time tomorrow, I'll give you a formal tour. It'll be better in any case on Sunday when the church is full and everyone on their best behaviour.'

'I could do with a little best behaviour,' Jennie mumbled, and then catching Piero's querying look, added warmly, 'I do hope you'll manage the time.'

The bittersweet drink finished, they strolled out into the warm night air. Jennie was surprised at how quickly it had turned dark, but a crescent moon and stars cast a dim glow over the road. The stillness, after the sounds of the hotel, seemed acute. Yet after a moment, Jennie could make out a cacophony of insects, busy in the hedges and orchards that bordered the road. If she listened carefully, their noise became deafening.

Piero seemed to read her thoughts. 'People always say the country is quiet, but I've never found it so.' He took her arm, gently guiding her along the side of the road, saying little until a bend brought all of Cefalu into their line of vision.

The village, which seemed to be hewn out of stone, jutted out into the sea. Its lights played merrily over a small harbour crowded with fishing boats. As if from nowhere the sounds of voices, the barking of dogs, the revving of motorbikes echoed around them, growing out of the hush as if an invisible curtain which separated town from country had suddenly been lifted. Piero laughed, 'Everyone's out—it's Saturday night and warm. There's nothing like an Italian town for street life.'

They made their way past a large square over which a church presided, down a narrow cobblestoned lane. In front of each house, people were sitting out on chairs, chatting, the woman sewing, the children playing noisily. One of the houses had a lantern hanging over its threshold and announced a *trattoria*.

'This is the place Derek recommended. Best in town,' Piero explained. Jennie stiffened at the sound of the name. 'Cold?' Piero wound his arm round her shoulders and guided her into a softly-lit room already crowded with people. The walls were brightly decorated with figures of robust fishermen tangling with outlandish fish, all painted with a bold naïve brush.

Jennie laughed, 'It's lovely—I'd love to cut one out and take him home.'

'I didn't know I was dining with a collector,' Piero grinned. 'If you're that way inclined, you'll want to take home half the island. It's dotted with naïve painters not to mention wonderful ceramicists, woodworkers, the lot.'

'I can't wait . . . though I imagine the only thing I'll manage to take home is a tan!'

A small sturdy waiter showed them to a table in an arched alcove and brought them two menus painted with figures resembling those on the walls.

'Perhaps I'll settle for one of these as a souvenir,' Jennie smiled, and set herself to deciphering the Italian menu.

'Would you like to try some *calamari*?' Piero asked. 'Not terribly English, but excellent here.'

'I'll try anything once.'

Piero winked at her, 'Bold lady! And very pretty too.' He examined her critically. 'Funny how you seem more relaxed here, more approachable than I've ever seen you in London. On the set you always wore an invisible hands off sign.'

Jennie flushed. 'It must be the weather,' she mumbled.

He eyed her quizzically for a moment and noting her embarrassment only said softly, 'Well, I'm glad it's gone.'

'I think I am too.' Jennie murmured, fingering the soft material of her shirt.

Piero gave their order to the waiter who had now approached their table. But his attention strayed from them as the clamour in the room suddenly gave way to an expectant hush, and Jennie looked up from her menu to see Daniela striding towards them, looking every inch the star she was in a silky black off-the-shoulder dress. She trailed a rainbow-coloured shawl indolently behind her, like some southern Garbo. All eyes in the room were on her and she played dramatically to the crowd, a wide smile on her face as she nodded greetings. Behind her came Derek, seemingly unbothered by the eyes that paid him equal due. Cast in the role of audience, Jennie saw him now as others must see him, a tall handsome man with beautifully mobile features, a man at home in his skin, ready to confront whatever was at hand, his presence charged with an electricity equal to Daniela's. She cast her eyes down on her plate, shivering a little as the mixed events of that afternoon came back to her: Derek pulling her out of the water, stretched out beside her on the sand, legs entwined with hers on the bed, Daniela's intrusion.

Suddenly he was looming over her, his voice demanding attention. 'Hello, Piero—hello, Jennie, shall we join you? There seem to be no empty tables.' Jennie's powers of speech disappeared somewhere into her fluttering stomach as she gazed into the steely blue of his eyes. 'Or would you prefer to be quite alone?' he queried cynically.

Daniela curled her arm through his, saving the need for reply. 'I'm sure they would prefer to be alone, Derek, so they can get to know each other a little better.' Her voice was insinuating.

'*Per la signora* Colombi, we can always find a table if she wishes,' the waiter intervened.

Daniela smiled her acknowledgment. 'Perhaps we can sit with you for a moment until our table is ready, yes?'

Jennie nodded and Daniela slipped down on the chair beside her, while Derek moved next to Piero.

'Well, Jennie, you seem quite recovered from this afternoon's adventure, altogether recovered.' There was a mocking light in Derek's eyes as they roved over her face. 'In fact, if it weren't a trifle cruel to suggest it, I might even say it had done you good.'

Jennie's dark eyes flashed anger. 'Perhaps I should take up being accosted professionally—only within saving distance, of course. It gives men the rare opportunity of being heroes. Oh yes, I can see the ad now. "Distressed damsel offers services to potential heroes. Prove your brawn for a small fee." ' Her voice dripped irony.

'Did something happen to you this afternoon, Jennie?' Piero's voice was low.

She turned to him. 'Two youths decided to flirt with me a little aggressively in the water. They took me by surprise, and I think I panicked.'

'And Derek saved her,' Daniela burst in, laughing. 'It seems to have gone to his head, this show of valour!'

'Well, next time I'll just stand by and enjoy the sight. Let you ladies fend for yourselves, if that's the way you prefer it.'

'Not me, *per Dio*,' Daniela exclaimed. 'You can save my life any time,' she directed a languorous gaze at Derek.

'Any time may be an exaggeration,' Jennie uttered curtly, and then seeing the hurt in his eyes, she mellowed, 'but I am grateful for today.'

He gave her a black look as the waiter came to usher them to their own table.

Piero looked at Jennie silently for a long moment. 'Were you in trouble this afternoon?' he asked at last.

She nodded. 'And Derek did help. I don't know what made me act so ungraciously. I guess it was just his manner,' she shrugged.

Piero eyed her sceptically. 'He's a good man, you know. One of the best I've worked with. And his patience with Daniela is extraordinary.'

Jennie flushed in embarrassment, sensing his rebuke. 'I know that. I'm sorry.'

'Is there something going on between the two of you?' His voice was gentle, friendly, but demanded an honest answer.

Jennie played nervously with her hair and then forced her eyes to meet Piero's. 'I don't know. He—well, he makes me uncomfortable.' The flush was still on her face.

Piero chuckled, 'Well, that's a promising beginning. But never mind about all that now. Let's enjoy this food.'

The waiter had set down two plates of *calamari* smelling invitingly of garlic and herbs. Jennie realised that she was starving. She returned Piero's warm smile. 'Thanks for being so patient with me. And for feeding me for the second, or is it the third time today.'

'I can't think of anyone I'd rather feed, my strange little prickly Englishwoman.'

'A strangely ravenous Englishwoman would be more like it!' Jennie laughed, and dug into the spicy food.

Dinner passed pleasantly now that they were alone and Jennie found herself basking in Piero's easy humour. Odd, she thought to herself as she watched him paying the bill, he feels like a friend. She grimaced inwardly, the only one I've made in years, apart from Mrs Owen.

Piero seemed to read her thoughts. 'These plane jour-
neys have a way of bringing people together in a hurry. If
you ever need a shoulder, Jennie, mine's quite broad. You
sometimes seem to need one desperately.'

She looked at him seriously. 'Thanks, I'll remember that.'

Only as they were leaving the restaurant did she once
again sense Derek's presence, the hard glint of his mocking
eyes which seemed to strip her bare. She allowed herself
to lean into the comfort of Piero's guiding arm. Sensing
her tension mingled with tiredness, he held her close and
gave her a comforting smile.

As she snuggled into the cool sheets that night, Jennie
was pleased at the thought of Piero's warmth, the burgeon-
ing friendship between them. But as an image of Derek
gazing at the two of them flitted over her eyelids, she felt
strangely at odds. It filled her with a sense of intoxicated
anticipation, sent a tremor through her limbs. Simultaneously, a nagging familiar voice surfaced within her,
issued warnings, telling her about the desirability of keeping herself only to herself. She sighed and sleep overcame
her before she could make sense of her warring emotions.

The next morning Jennie got out of bed with a flush of
exhilaration. A whole day of sun and sea awaited her.
She poked Kathy recklessly awake. 'Fancy coming down
to the beach with me? I don't want to waste another
second indoors.'

Kathy rolled over muttering and then climbed out of
bed. 'For a minute, I'd forgotten where we were. Yes,
please, lead the way ... but can we stop for a cup of
coffee first?' She wiped the sleep from her eyes.

Jennie grinned, 'If it's a brief pause.' She rummaged
through her drawers and case for her swimming suit and
groaned, 'Blast! I left my bikini in Derek's room.'

Kathy looked at her curiously.

'It's not what you think,' Jennie hastened to say. 'But
what do I do now? Is it too early to knock at his door?'

Kathy glanced at the travelling alarm clock by her bed. 'Nine-thirty. Almost a civilised hour.'

Jennie garnered her courage. The temptation to swim was enormous. But could she face knocking at Derek's door? And what if he weren't alone?

'I'd lend you one of mine, but it would float on you,' Kathy offered.

Jennie shook her head. 'I'll go and knock very softly.' She splashed some cold water over her face, pulled on shorts and a tee-shirt and throwing her shoulders back marched out of the room.

She knocked quietly at Derek's door, waited no more than a second and began to turn away. Just then the door opened and Derek's broad shoulders filled the doorway. He was clad in sparkling white and looked thoroughly composed, a sheaf of notes in one hand.

'Well, this is an unexpected pleasure,' he said softly, only a hint of irony in his voice as he ushered her into the room.

Jennie demurred. 'I left my swimsuit here yesterday,' her lips trembled a little as she said it, 'and I wanted to go for a swim . . .'

His eyes twinkled. 'Bad habit, leaving your clothes in men's rooms.'

'It's hardly a habit,' Jennie replied heatedly.

'Come in and have some coffee while I go and look for it. And do try to be gracious for a few minutes with the man who saved your life,' he chuckled, and Jennie walked into the room, sitting down by the little table where a pot of coffee stood invitingly.

'Pour yourself some,' Derek ordered.

Jennie did, and sipped its hot fragrance, letting her eyes roam around the room. The large double bed was thoroughly tumbled and she looked away from it quickly.

Derek caught her glance. 'I'm a restless sleeper,' he said casually. He pulled a strand of hair away from her eyes. 'Perhaps you can come and calm me down one night.'

Jennie could think of nothing to say in return, but she moved away from his touch as if from an arching flame. She sipped her coffee quickly and having emptied the cup, asked again for her bikini.

Derek went into the bathroom and came back with it. 'I hope you're not planning to venture out alone today,' he said menacingly, and then added more kindly, 'I'd offer you my protection, but I have some work to finish up. Perhaps I'll join you later. In fact there was something I wanted to ask your opinion on.'

Jennie hid her surprise and simply nodded her thanks, leaving the room as quickly as she could. But she wondered what it was Derek could possibly want to know of her.

There were already a few of the team on the little cove beach when Jennie and Kathy arrived. Tempted by the sight of the lounging bodies, Jennie took out her sketchpad and withdrew to a perch she noticed on one of the boulders. Here she sketched happily until the sun's heat impelled her towards the sea.

She plunged in, revelling in the water's smoothness, and swam out fearlessly towards a rock she could make out in the distance. She rested for a moment on its slippery surface and then swam back, stretching out on the sand by Kathy's side. The sun beat down on her with its powerful rays, cleansing her of the last remnants of strained anxiety, searing out the restless little voice of her anxious will.

A shadow falling over her face stirred her eyes open. She looked up to find Derek standing over her, his lithe frame a glistening golden brown in the strong sunlight.

'Fancy another swim?' The deep blue of his eyes emitted a magnetic pull.

Jennie rose lazily. 'Mmm, that would be nice.'

They raced into the sea together splashing froth from the waves. Derek laughed, 'Race you to the rock!'

Jennie exerted herself, but she was no match for him.

His clean powerful strokes brought him to the distant rock with no visible exertion. She came up beside him and his strong arms lifted her easily on to the rock.

'I've got an unfair advantage,' he smiled. 'Years of California.'

'Against my years at the local swimming baths.' She looked up at him, suddenly shy as she took in the rugged beauty of the man poised on the boulder between sea and sky.

His eyes flickered sensuously over her body and he put out a hand to touch her thigh. Jennie flinched away, and Derek's smile grew devilish. 'Do you trust yourself to do a little sightseeing with me?'

Jennie glared at his emphasis. 'I'm the *only* one I trust,' she said, so acutely aware of his presence that she wasn't sure of the truth of her words. 'But I can never refuse a sight,' she added with an attempt at levity.

He raised an eyebrow in amusement. 'Let's go, then.' He dived gracefully into the water, his arms cleaving the waves, then slowing to match his stroke to Jennie's. They reached the shore together, Jennie panting a little as her sea-borne limbs grew heavy on land.

She walked towards Kathy and noticed how she was gazing at Derek in open admiration. 'Lucky you!' she whispered as Jennie approached.

Derek followed, his taut muscles rippling golden as he moved. He dropped down next to Jennie and noticing her sketchpad picked it up and flicked through it.

'I see you're hard at work on bodies again,' he said mockingly.

'But not yours, you'll note,' she replied, her eyes darting anger as she took in his implied criticism.

'It's available, at least for the moment.' His smile was wry.

'But I'm not,' Jennie retorted, flushing.

'Oh, Jennie, do a quick sketch of Derek and me,' Kathy pleaded.

'I'm not a photographer, Kathy,' Jennie laughed a little stiffly. 'I need a little inspiration.'

'Which we don't provide,' Derek said mischievously, 'as I know from harsh experience.' He put his arm around Kathy's shoulder. 'Though I must say, I do find you rather inspiring, Kathy.'

Jennie felt her skin grow cold despite the hot sun as she followed the course of Derek's arm.

'Yes, perhaps in that pose, you do inspire me.' Jennie's voice was crisp. She dried her hands and reached for her pad and pencil.

With quick sure strokes she drew a caricature of Derek, bemuscled, arrogant, ridiculous he-man, arms around a voluptuous blonde whose cleavage he was leering into. A balloon floating out of his mouth read, 'I so love your mind, darling.' Jennie boxed the image in postcard-fashion and underneath wrote 'Souvenir of Sicily.' She tore the page abruptly out of her pad and flung it laughingly at Derek. 'There!' She turned to Kathy and whispered, 'I'll do a proper portrait of you later.'

Derek studied the picture for a moment, then burst into laughter. 'Nice to know how you see me! With your permission, Kathy, I'll send this to that grandmother I keep telling Jennie about. It will relieve her. She thinks I'm just a dull intellectual, but this lady, with true artistic insight, knows I'm not.' He looked at Jennie with an exaggerated ogle, letting his eyes move sensuously over her body.

Jennie said nothing, merely reached for her shorts and top and pulled them over her slender form to hide it a little from his eyes.

Derek rose, 'I guess it's time to investigate those promised sights,' and before Jennie could reply, he had said goodbye to Kathy and was following her up the slope towards the hotel.

'So I'm a ridiculous, empty-headed, womanising beach-boy, am I?' he said sternly as they moved out of earshot.

'And you I suppose see yourself as Diana, untouchable goddess of soulful purity.' He gripped her shoulder fiercely, forcing her to turn towards him. Then with barely perceptible pressure he slowly traced the line of her wide lips, moving his fingers down her throat to the arch of her bosom.

Jennie felt her blood pounding ominously through her veins, her legs growing weak.

'Why is it, then, O chaste and stern goddess, that you respond so avidly to my merest touch?' His voice was cruel.

Jennie pulled away and ran up the path, her cheeks flushed in humiliation.

He stopped her. 'I was just returning your barbed compliment,' he said quietly. 'Each one to his own weapons, you know. Now we can start again. Go and get changed and we'll do that long-awaited sightseeing.'

Jennie raced away, glad of the momentary respite. Without allowing herself to think, she showered the sea off herself and changed into white trousers and a halter top. Her skin was turning a rosy brown and her face in the mirror looked flushed with health. Whatever she might be feeling, she noted, her appearance was obviously blossoming. She gave herself a reassuring little smile and ran down the stairs, not bothering to wait for the lift.

Derek was waiting in front of the hotel. He opened the car door to her and they pulled off towards Cefalu.

'Not too long a tour today, because I'll have to get back. But I imagine you haven't yet had time to take in all the local sights.'

'Whatever I did see was in the dark, and it certainly didn't look like this.' Jennie leaned well back in her seat and took in the surrounding country, a wide smile on her face. The sun, now almost at its zenith, created a haze around everything. In the stillness, the heavily laden lemon trees seemed unable to stir and the bright little wildflowers that bordered the road melted into a single blaze of colour.

Cefalu was before them in minutes, its headland jutting out across a corn-blue bay, like some giant prehistoric fish basking in the sun. Derek parked the car just outside the town.

'Right, which shall it be today, pagan or Christian?' he asked, turning to her.

For a moment she was too struck by the craggy beauty of his face beneath the thickly tousled golden hair to reply. 'Pagan,' she breathed finally, feeling the word leave her lips with a flavour of danger.

His eyes smiled, reflecting the blue of the sea. 'More arduous to get to, but well worth the effort.' He led her along the side of the road to a narrow path that climbed steeply up the headland. She followed, glad of his arm and of the old trees which provided momentary respite from the blazing sun. They talked little, saving their energy for the sharp incline, occasionally straying off on to sheltered little trails ripe with greenery. When they reached the top, Jennie gasped in childlike delight. There before them was a breathtaking coastal panorama, stretching for miles and receding only where sea met horizon. Derek wound his arm round her shoulder and when she had gazed her fill led her away from the vista to a picturesque medieval ruin. In the midst of it stood a structure which seemed quite different from the rest.

Derek winked at her mischievously. 'Welcome to the Temple of Diana, Miss Lewis. Would you like to offer a sacrifice, pay some token homage?'

Jennie bridled at the mockery in his tone. Impetuously she turned towards him, ran a finger over his lips and pressed her mouth to his. When she felt his surprise recede into response, she pulled away and, to her astonishment as much as his, slapped him hard.

His eyes grew dangerously dark, as he rubbed his cheek. 'You little wildcat!' he muttered.

She stood her ground. 'You asked for homage—well, I pay mine to Diana the huntress,' she said in a cold voice.

He reached for her arm, but she evaded his grasp and ran willy-nilly down the hill, stopping only when the tears blinded her eyes.

He was right behind her and pulled her towards him roughly, his jaw clenched. 'Don't ever do that again,' he said in an icy tone. Then, as he took in her tears, the tight line of his mouth relaxed a little. 'If you want me to drive you back now, I will. Alternatively,' he paused, 'we could have a bite to eat together.'

Afraid to meet his eyes, Jennie searched in her bag for a tissue. The thought flashed through her mind that she really couldn't bear to be alone and confront the enormity of her impetuous gesture. She found her sunglasses and stalling for time perched them on her nose. Randomly she plucked a small blue flower from the side of the path and gave it to him.

'You make me do the most extraordinary things,' she said at last, finding a tone which hid the jumble of her emotions. She looked up at him and shook her head in wonder. 'I'm really a nice straightforward, rather serious person.'

A smile spread slowly over his rugged features and abandoned itself in full-bodied laughter. Like the sun bursting through a stormcloud, Jennie thought irrelevantly.

'Well, I think I can cope with a nice straightforward, rather serious person. Will you introduce me over lunch? I might have something to discuss with her.'

They made their way along narrow stepped streets, devoid of sunlight and refreshingly cool, like the interstices of some Arab town. A few minutes' walk led them to the church square, banked by cafés. Here they sat down and Jennie feasted her eyes on the graceful cathedral.

'It's one of the finest examples of that singularly Sicilian mixture of Norman, Byzantine and Spanish Baroque,'

Derek offered. 'Sicily somehow managed to take the best of every culture that invaded it.'

'Tell me more,' Jennie urged, sipping a little of the cool white wine the waiter had placed in front of them.

Derek chuckled. 'Well, let's see. I haven't read my guide book recently, but I think the first king of Sicily, Roger II, had the cathedral built. They started some time in the twelfth century, 1131 if I remember precisely,' he flashed her a wry smile. 'It took over a century to complete, and so,' he gestured towards the church, 'the mixture of styles you see in front of you. One of the later kings vowed to have the cathedral finished. He was nearly shipwrecked on the headland and it was a customary way of expressing thanks. Quite unlike the homage you offered to Diana,' he added sardonically.

Jennie flung him a wary look from beneath lowered lids, but he was still smiling. 'Far more lasting in any case. I wish I had time to sketch it.'

'Feel free. I'm quite happy just to sit. And watch, if that's permitted.'

She shook her head. 'No, I'll come back during the week, if there's time. Piero said he'd show me round.'

Derek's jaw suddenly tightened. 'For a woman who pretends not to like men, you have your guides well picked out.'

'Oh, there's an endless stream of them,' Jennie quipped flippantly. Then giving him a taunting smile, she excused herself and went in search of a ladies' room. She felt the need to be on her own for a moment, away from the searching intensity of Derek's appraisal. The interior of the café was a large almost bare room, simply furnished with wooden tables and chairs. At the back, she found a sign pointing the way to a rather primitive W.C. She splashed cold water on her face, passed a brush through her tangled sea-dry hair and looked at herself in the crooked slit of a mirror. It returned a stranger's face with flashing dark eyes set in sunwarmed skin. Even the expression was unrecognisable, somehow bolder, more direct.

Jennie shrugged at this other woman who seemed unafraid of life and walked out of the café into the bright light of the terrace. A group of sultry-eyed young men lounging around a nearby table eyed her brazenly as she passed. One rose from his seat and gestured for her to join them. Jennie shook her head and strode away, almost colliding with Derek.

'In need of my protective powers again?' he queried.

Jennie laughed. 'The protection racket seems to be endemic around here! Still, you don't strike me as a godfather.'

'Thank heaven for small mercies,' Derek laughed. 'I couldn't face another cartoon from you.'

They sat down, just as the waiter placed two plates of *fritto misto* in front of them. Jennie breathed in the sea smell and then bit into the crispy fish morsels. 'Delicious!' she exclaimed. 'Do you know, I think I shall leave here looking like a buxom Italian *mamma*.'

'You have a long way to go, young lady,' Derek muttered, glancing at her slender form. As his eyes skimmed over her, Jennie suddenly felt an ache forming in her, a desire to pass her fingers over his chest, its proportions so beautifully moulded by his brilliantly white shirt. She pushed the thought aside and forced her eyes downward to her plate.

They ate in silence for a while and then Derek began to tell her of the perfect sites he had discovered for the film. They would begin shooting exteriors tomorrow. His brow furrowed in concentration as he warmed to his subject and Jennie found herself remembering what she had all but forgotten in the sheer excitement of his animal presence: here was a man of incisive intelligence, thoroughly dedicated to his work. All at once she felt humble, stupidly young. She listened carefully to all that he he said, and by the time coffee came, she felt strangely privileged.

It was then that Derek turned to her, a new note of seriousness in his tone. 'Jennie, do you remember earlier today I said I wanted your opinion on something?'

She nodded, now intensely curious about what he might say.

'It's a little unprofessional and a little complicated,' he paused, 'but here goes. You know those wonderful old Etruscan tomb paintings?'

'Yes,' Jennie murmured, wondering what he was leading up to.

'Well, I'd set a scene in one of the reconstructed tombs. But because of the expense involved in going to another location, now that we're running behind schedule, Matthew wants to cut the scene out or set it elsewhere. I thought of trying to find someone here who could recreate it cheaply and quickly, but haven't had any luck. Then it occurred to me that you with that wonderful quick hand of yours . . .' He stopped and looked at her questioningly.

'I'm not quite sure what you're getting at,' Jennie said honestly.

'Well, I thought you might be able to copy or at least render the visual feel of one of those tombs. Do you think it's possible?'

'Oh, I see!' Jennie breathed deeply. 'Directly on to a wall.'

Derek nodded. 'I found just the place—even as to the proportions of the arches. And in the car, I've a book full of magnificent reproductions. Do you think you could have a go, Jennie?' His face held a mixture of challenge and pleading.

'I can't promise any marvellous results——' Jennie hesitated and then smiled broadly, 'but I'll try. I've done some scene painting before, if that's any use.'

His blue eyes flashed pleasure. 'Good, I had a feeling I could count on you. Shall we go and have a look at the place now? I can have whatever materials you need brought from Palermo in the morning.' He was suddenly all activity, hailing the waiter, paying the bill, all but running Jennie through the narrow streets to the car.

'But wait a minute, Derek—what about work? Real work, like making up Daniela,' Jennie found herself stumbling over the name. 'That begins tomorrow. I can't very well . . .'

Derek cut her off in mid-sentence. 'Don't worry, I'll see to all that. Meanwhile feast your eyes on this.' He took a large sumptuously illustrated volume out of the car's boot and opened it at a marked page.

Jennie took in the image: two youths with darkly hooded eyes, their bodies all but floating on an arch's curve. 'I can only try,' she reiterated.

'Good lady!' Derek seemed ready to embrace her and then stopped himself, taking her hand instead and squeezing it firmly. 'Do you think it can be done in a day?'

Jennie gulped and repeated, 'I can only try.'

Derek smiled and urged her into the car. He drove smoothly up a snaking road towards a cluster of houses set amidst olive groves. 'Here we are.' He ushered her towards one of the houses, introduced her effusively, from what Jennie could understand, to the lady of the house, who led them to an outlying building. It seemed to be a storehouse of some kind, but Jennie noted that the curves of the walls were closely reminiscent of the picture Derek had shown her.

'I've told her you're a famous English artist,' Derek whispered to her, a chuckle in his voice. 'Who knows, perhaps I'm right, only slightly ahead of time.'

Jennie flushed and concentrated on noting the proportions of the store room. Suddenly she was itching to begin.

'Can you get that book again, Derek?' she surprised herself with her own tone of command.

He eyed her strangely. 'Do you want to start now?'

She shook her head. 'No, only get the feel of the thing.'

But when he brought the book back and turned to the relevant image, she thought she might just do a quick outline in preparation for the morrow's work. She dug into her bag for a stick of charcoal and becoming almost oblivious of the others, started to do some hasty scaling and draw rough outlines on the wall.

When she finished, she turned and noticed Derek's look of admiration. 'I knew you could do it, Jennie!' His eyes were warm on her. All at once she grew selfconscious, awkward in her movements. She struggled away from the arm he tried to place round her.

'I can't do much more, until I get proper materials.'

He nodded and led her towards the car. 'Just tell me what you need and by nine tomorrow morning it will all be waiting for you.'

Jennie slid into the car, glad that there was something particular to discuss. She was surprised to hear Derek talking of paints and washes with almost professional know-how and she looked at him curiously.

'I've done my homework,' he offered, noting her amazement and smiling at her from the blue depths of his eyes.

The atmosphere between them was suddenly easy. In a strange way they had become equals, part of a team, and Jennie found herself uttering a silent prayer that it might last.

But as they pulled up at the hotel, her heart sank. Daniela was immediately upon them.

'Where have you been, Derek? I've been looking everywhere for you!' Daniela's voice was plaintive and she gave Jennie a grudging glance as she took hold of Derek's arm possessively.

'Am I late?' Derek looked at his watch and dismissed Daniela's question.

'Giancarlo has been waiting impatiently for you to take him for a swim.'

A small boy with Daniela's large eyes, but in a shade of

velvety brown, came up to Derek and shyly took hold of his hand. Derek put his large arm protectively round his shoulder and bent to whisper something in his ear. A wide smile broke out over the boy's solemn face. Daniela laughed and, maternal pride overcoming mistrust, she motioned to Jennie.

'Come and meet my Giancarlo. Isn't he glorious?' She gave the lad a joyful hug, tickling him as he tried to squirm out of her arms. Then, in Italian, she introduced him to Jennie. The boy looked at her with his wide serious eyes and shook her hand politely. But it was all too clear that his interest was in Derek and he turned away from the women as soon as he could to tug at the man's arm.

Derek grinned, ruffling the boy's thick hair, and then lifted him up over his shoulder with an exaggerated groan of effort. He nodded distractedly at Jennie, said a quick, 'See you tomorrow,' and turned towards the lift, chatting away to the lad who burst into giggles.

'Giancarlo adores him,' said Daniela, shaking her head, but obviously delighted; and giving Jennie a meaningful look, she followed after Derek.

Well, that's that, Jennie said to herself. I've been roundly dismissed. A hard ball of indignation formed inside her. By the time she had reached her room, it had exploded into helpless rage. She flung her bag aside vehemently, tore off her trousers and sprawled on the bed. 'Private Property'—Daniela had clearly constructed a wall around Derek and put up her signpost. And except for random little excursions, fleeting escapades, not to mention making use of her when necessary, Derek seemed quite happy within the walls. Jennie pounded her pillow with her fists as humiliation welled up in her, finally finding its vent in tears. But why should you care? the nagging little familiar voice inside her asked, just treat him as dismissively as he treats you. Enjoy the moments, even the sensual ones. But keep yourself to yourself.

I can't, Jennie wailed in reply. A thought she had been

afraid to face suddenly crystallised in her mind. I think
I'm falling in love with him.

It was an emotion unlike any she had experienced
before, even with Max. It was like what she had read
about in books and contemptuously termed fantasy. And
as she realised its obsessive power, the fact that she was
not altogether her own person any more, she flung her
pillow across the room and buried her hot face in her
arms.

CHAPTER SEVEN

THE next morning it was an early rise and Jennie could feel the hotel bristling with activity. By seven o'clock, she was the only one left in the large dining room, the others having all disappeared, presumably to the location site. She sipped her black coffee with mounting impatience, wondering whether Derek would really be back at the given time with the promised materials. After half an hour of dawdling, she grew too restless to sit any longer. Perhaps she had dreamt up the whole scheme as a way of bringing Derek closer to her. No one else on the team seemed to know anything about it and they had cast her odd looks, or so it seemed to her, when she had lingered behind.

Stop that, Jennie! she scolded herself. You've been asked to do a job of work, that's certain. Now just think about that. She determined on a swim to pass the time. Slipping quickly into her bikini, she went down to the beach and plunged in, not bothering to look around her. She swam to the rock she had perched on with Derek, and then with a sudden lunge veered away from it. No point deliberately stirring up memories of his touch; it was bad enough waiting for him to appear. She floated aimlessly on her back, watching the pale clarity of the morning sky, and then with a crisp backstroke made her way to the deserted beach. She dried herself briskly and throwing the towel over her shoulders, walked back up the path to the hotel.

Half way there, she saw Derek's lithe form moving towards her, and sighed with unconscious relief. She hadn't dreamt the whole thing up.

'Thought I might find you here tempting the fates

again,' he said as he came up to her. He shook his head in mock desperation.

Jennie felt herself flush. She had all but forgotten her recent struggle with the youths. She shrugged the matter away and asked pointedly, 'Did you manage to get the materials?'

Derek smiled his warm smile. Funny, Jennie thought to herself, how he can look so dangerously arrogant one minute, and then the next be so likeable.

'You're raring to get started, aren't you? Well, let's go. Everything's in the car.'

She hurried up to her room to change and met him at the front of the hotel minutes later. He seemed to be startled by her appearance.

'I didn't expect you down so quickly.'

Jennie found herself laughing. 'We don't all take as long as Daniela,' the words slipped out before she had a chance to censor them.

He threw her an oddly troubled glance and then muttered under his breath, 'Touché!'

They drove swiftly, smoothly, through sun-filled groves and stopped by the cluster of houses, their windows shuttered to the sun. Derek carried the materials towards the small storehouse. 'I'm going to have to leave you here and run. They're expecting me on location. But I'll try to get back later in the day to see how you're getting on.'

Jennie nodded.

'I'll ask our hostess to see to some lunch for you.' He set the materials together with the book of Etruscan reproductions down for her in a corner of the room. 'Work well,' he said, and then, hesitating as he walked towards the door, he brushed her hair with his lips. 'And thanks.'

Jennie shivered, made a conscious effort to push her emotions to one side, and focussed her attention on the Etruscan image. She sized it up carefully now and set to work, stopping only for a brief moment for a bite of lunch. By mid-afternoon, the figures were all but done and her legs and arms were aching from the sheer continuous effort. She put down her brush and went out for a breath of air. At the end of the narrow tree-lined path, she all but collided with Derek.

'Finished?' He looked amazed.

'Not quite,' Jennie laughed. 'Just stretching my legs. But come and have a look for yourself.'

He followed her into the dimmer light of the store room and after a second exclaimed in delight. 'Jennie, you're wonderful! You've done it!' He caught her up in his strong arms and lifted her off the floor, twirling her round and round in sheer exuberance. When he put her down, she looked up at him breathlessly, accidentally catching his gaze. Suddenly his arms were round her with a different intensity and his lips covered hers in a long kiss. Then gently he drew away. 'Thank you, Jennie,' he whispered.

She found herself wondering whether he was referring to her work or to the slow pleasure of their kiss.

'I'm going to have to go again now—unfortunately,' he grimaced. 'I'd much rather watch you. But I'll send a car round to pick you up. When do you think you'll be through?'

Jennie shrugged and turned away from him, suddenly irritated. 'In a couple of hours, I guess.'

'Good.' She felt his hand on her shoulder and he was gone, calling a, 'See you later!'

Jennie returned to her painting, but her concentration was now broken. Images of Derek flitted through her mind and she was unable to chase them away. They all focussed on a single point of expectation: she would see him again that evening.

But she didn't. When she returned to the hotel, he was nowhere in sight. Nor did he appear in the bar during the course of the evening. And the following day it was back to the bustle of work of another kind, with little time left for any thought: a six o'clock call, a rushed breakfast, and then off in vans and buses to the mountain town of

Cacomo which Derek and Matthew had chosen as home
base for their peasant family. Jennie clutched the large
make-up bag to her as the bus made its way to the interior
of the island, veering round sharp bends in the steep road.
Orchards gave way to fields carpeted in a profusion of
wild flowers. It was hard in this springtime of the year to
believe what Piero had said to her about Sicily's major
problem: infertile land combined with a highly fertile
population. But if she shut her eyes she could imagine the
thick beds of flowers shrivelling away under the blazing
sun and leaving scorched dry earth. The film script she
knew talked of families on the starvation line, heads of
households who earned their keep by gathering snails or
herbs as the season demanded; entire villages without
doctors or schools; peasants paying rent to distant land-
owners, a rent enforced by gangs of armed men who laid
the basis for the Mafia.

She shrugged as she thought of the misery all this
natural beauty veiled. The bus chugged slowly across a
narrow bridge beneath which a deep ravine gaped, rivu-
lets pouring down its side. A few more minutes and a
bend in the road displayed a steep mountain town,
perched in grey-white solitude atop an elephantine slope.
The bus pulled up behind the vans and they piled out.
Jennie felt a stiff dust-filled breeze whip her hair across
her face as she followed the crew up a street which was in
reality a dirt path. It led between a row of grey stone
houses which seemed to grow higgledy-piggledy out of the
earth. Lines of washing flapped in the wind with a strange
whipping sound. Dark-eyed urchins came out of the
houses to watch them pass and behind the shutters Jennie
sensed the fixed staring eyes of women clothed in heavy
black. An occasional ragged chicken clucked at them
nervously and strayed across their path. To the sides of
the houses, goats tied to posts gazed at them with calm
unblinking eyes. The air echoed with the crowing of roos-
ters, quite uninterested in the time of day.

Jennie and Kathy were ushered into a house which was to serve as their work quarters. A cool dark room clear of anything but a table and some straightbacked chairs standing stiffly by the walls had evidently been prepared for them. An olive carved crucifix and a brightly painted Madonna served as the only ornaments. Jennie and Kathy placed their bags on the stone floor and turned to shake hands with a plump woman in a loose print dress who seemed to be the mistress of the house. She was trailed by three small ragamuffins who escaped from behind their mother's skirts to tug at Kathy and Jennie. Jennie reached into her bag and brought out some sweets which she handed to the children after the mother had nodded approval. Smiles beamed the children's faces and they protested as their mother scuttled them out of the room. They refused to go further than the doorway, gaping at the strangers' every movement with bright eyes.

A stern male voice intervened to order them away. Jennie tried to gesture that the children's presence wouldn't disturb them. The owner of the voice came in to greet them and explain that the children were better off out of doors. Much to Jennie and Kathy's surprise, he spoke in accented but distinct American English. He was an old man whose taut brown skin was etched with wrinkles. When they expressed relief that he spoke English, he explained that in his youth he had lived in the United States. Jennie and Kathy smiled at each other.

'A little eerie how all this duplicates our script exactly,' Jennie whispered to Kathy when he had left the room.

'Derek obviously did his homework,' said Kathy, just as their host returned with two cups of bitterly strong coffee. They thanked him and Jennie set to work arranging her supplies on the table. She had only just finished when she made out Daniela and Arno's voices outside the house. They came in, effusively greeting everyone, chucking the children under the chin. Behind them a crew member arrived carrying wardrobe cases.

Jennie set to work as soon as Kathy had finished dressing Daniela. There would be a lot of people to make up today and although she knew the work was being shared with some Italian crew members, it was still a hefty load.

'The shooting script calls for a young hag today, Jennie,' Daniela grimaced, 'so leave me as natural as you dare!'

Jennie tried a smile. Daniela was obviously in good spirits today. Yet Jennie couldn't prevent her own resentment from rising in her. She pulled Daniela's electric hair back more roughly than usual into a tight bun and then stopped her childish flare of temper and concentrated on her task. She made the actress up only minimally, toning her features down into an austere sensuality.

Daniela looked at herself in the small mirror Jennie had taken out of her case. 'Yes, that will do perfectly,' she said, obviously pleased at the result. 'I wonder how Giancarlo will like me. We brought him along for today's shooting. And my mother. You must meet her later, Jennie. Derek,' she added pointedly, 'is very fond of her.'

Daniela left, to be replaced by Arno and then a string of others. By ten o'clock when Jennie had finished her first round, she felt thoroughly drained. She walked out, startled by the glare of the bright sunlight after the shade of the house, and made for the crowd she saw a little distance away. All the women and children of the village seemed to be gathered round, the older ones knitting or sewing and pretending a stern lack of curiosity; the younger ones openly excited by the unusual events. In the distance on a rugged slope of hill, Jennie made out a group of men gathered as if for a public meeting, Arno in their midst waving his arms and declaiming. Jennie laughed. They made an odd spectacle, surrounded as they were by the numerous technicians. Artifice looked strangely more real here than reality. Much of the village,

Jennie realised, must be serving as extras. She looked round slowly. Little would have to be changed. There were no television aerials to take down, few cars to remove to ensure period flavour. Still caught in a distant moment of time, the village was a perfect location choice.

She wandered around a little aimlessly until she came upon Daniela rehearsing a scene with three small children, being put through their paces by Piero. They were gathering dandelions in a field, Daniela presumably instructing them as to the choicest. An older woman, but still very much in her prime, was standing next to Giancarlo and watching. From time to time she shouted instructions in a throaty voice to Daniela, who laughed.

When she saw Jennie, she stopped and called out, 'Meet my mother. She thinks she's replacing Matthew as director. It's true she knows more about dandelions, let alone about acting.'

The older woman turned and shook Jennie's hand. '*Bellissima!*' she exclaimed. 'You are the make-up lady Daniela has mentioned to me.' Her English was deliberately slow, but perfect, as if her tongue were remembering inflections. Jennie returned her smile and nodded. She immediately sensed she liked the older woman with her bold, open face, a casual but elegant print dress loosely clothing her girth.

'My daughter,' the older woman said conspiratorially, 'will be a good actress one of these days, perhaps when she stops being so, how do you say it in English, so sexy. But I think this is perhaps her best film. That Derek Hunter is an intelligent scriptwriter. There are not too many around these days.'

Giancarlo tugged at her arm as he heard the name Derek.

'The little one is impatient. Derek has promised to show him how one of the bandit's guns works. Perhaps you could show him what you carry around in your case, it will keep him occupied.'

Jennie opened her make-up case and in gestures asked Giancarlo if he would like to have some of the colours applied to his face. His grandmother amplified and the little boy's face broke into a wide grin. He shouted something excitely to his grandmother.

'He would like you to turn him into a bandit.'

'Why not?' said Jennie, and set herself to transforming the little boy into a melodramatic silent film version of a villain.

When she showed him his reflection in her small pocket mirror, he shouted with glee. Jennie found herself giggling at the sight and promising to return later, to wash off moustache and heavy eyebrows, she wandered towards the slope where the public meeting was being filmed. They might need her there. She covered the short distance to the site, being careful to keep well out of camera range, and found a perch on a grassy knoll nearby. As she looked around, she caught sight of Derek standing tall on the edges of the crowd. She had managed to keep him out of her mind since yesterday, but now as she saw him standing tall in snug jeans, his face intent in concentration, her heart lurched. She forced her eyes away on to the vista in front of her, and after a few minutes stood-up again to wander around restlessly. She must keep her mind off Derek. There was no question of even attempting to re-place Daniela in his affections. Daniela, who was so beautiful, so successful. And with that wonderful mother, Jennie thought suddenly. An image of her stepfather sprang to her mind from nowhere, engulfing her in shame. Yes, far better to keep herself away from Derek—if she could manage it—before she allowed herself to grow irre-vocably involved. It would minimise the pain of finding herself slighted by him.

She bumped into Kathy on one of the small paths lead-ing back to the village. 'Come and see the man who plays Daniela's grandson,' she said excitedly. 'He's exquisitely handsome.'

Jennie followed Kathy up the path to one of the village

houses in front of which Daniela and a young man were rehearsing one of the most important moments in the script. Jennie remembered it well from a preliminary reading. The grandson, a youth of about twenty, was a member of a terrorist group akin to the Red Brigade. He had moved from Sicily to some northern town, and in trouble, he had now come home. The scene showed him trying to explain, first to his grandmother and then to his grandfather, that in fact his ideas, even his actions, were a direct outgrowth of theirs. What he was fighting against and for was no different from what they had fought for.

Jennie looked at the youth's brooding eyes, the intensity of his features and gestures as he spoke to his grandmother; the restlessness of his movements as he paced in front of the house.

'Perfect casting,' she whispered to Kathy. 'He's ideal for the part.'

'And so dishy. One look from him and I'm a lost woman,' Kathy groaned theatrically. 'And I'm responsible for dressing him!'

They watched the scene intently and though it was being spoken in Italian, Jennie felt she understood every word. The actor's voice, she knew, would be dubbed in and synchronised later, like most of this location work.

She was so wrapped up in watching that it was only after the scene was over that she noticed Derek standing a little away from them. He went up to greet the actor and Daniela, and spoke rapidly to them in Italian. The young actor let out an abrupt laugh and clapped his hands together as if Derek had just given him some droll insight. Jennie watched for a moment longer and then withdrew to the cool of her room. Despite the resolutions she had made to herself earlier, she was piqued at Derek's total obliviousness to her presence. Better not to be near him, she determined again, as she sipped the cold drink her host proffered.

The next few days passed in a welter of activity. They

were up by six-thirty and never returned to the hotel before ten at night. Jennie felt drained, but grateful for the pressure which kept her mind occupied. She had taken to wearing her bikini under her clothes and every time there was a spare moment, she would slip away to some hidden nook and stretch out in the blazing sun, often with her sketchpad in hand. As she looked over her work at night, she felt quite pleased. Despite the lack of time, she had a good set of visual notes there. And on top of it, her skin had turned a rich nut brown. With her hair tossed by the sea wind thickly framing her fine-boned face, the whites of her eyes bright against her tanned skin, she looked in her mirror at night like some different creature, the child of some wild sunbaked mountain village, rather than a bleak northern town. She laughed at her own romanticism, but it didn't displease her.

It was only on the following Thursday that she again saw Derek face to face. He strode into the make-up room late in the afternoon when she was lotioning Arno's face clean. The room's proportions were suddenly dwarfed by his presence and Jennie felt a tremor run through her. She tried to still her trembling hands.

'How about taking off a little early and driving into Palermo with me? I've got some things to do there,' he said with no preliminary greeting.

'I don't know if I can leave yet,' Jennie demurred, steeling herself against him.

'It's all right. I've asked Paola if she'd stand in for you and she's agreed.'

Jennie bridled at his presumption, feeling irritated at rather than grateful to the Italian make-up supervisor whom she had met in the course of the week. She was angry too at the fact that Derek had not yet said anything about the completed wall painting. She finished cleansing Arno's face slowly, biding her time. At last she gathered her brushes and jars into her bag. 'Right, I'm ready,' she said with no enthusiasm in her voice.

He led her towards the car, and only when they were inside did he turn to face her. 'I never did thank you properly for your wonderful work. Matthew is quite prepared to keep the scene now. I'm enormously grateful, Jennie,' his eyes were warm on her face making her pulse race, 'enormously grateful,' he stressed, 'and I'm sorry I haven't had the time to thank you properly before.'

She lowered her eyes away from him, finding herself unable to respond, now that he had said precisely what she wanted to hear.

He drove the car skilfully along the bumpy road and then picked up speed. 'I thought we'd stop at the hotel for a wash and change of clothes, and then head off. I'll take you out for a splendid dinner, by way of thanks.'

Jennie still could find nothing to say. Her voice seemed to be a barometer of her pulse, one vanishing as the other increased. And now that she was again alone with him in the car's small space and could see his rugged profile from beneath lowered lids, feel him but a few inches away from her, her heart raced more quickly than the car's engine. Determinedly she looked ahead of her, trying to think of conversational titbits. But her mind was blank. When they reached the less treacherous coastal road, Derek's hand strayed along the car seat in search of hers.

'I seem to have seen nothing of you these days. Have you been hiding?'

Jennie shook her head and roughly extricated her hand from his, afraid of the welter of emotions and sensations his touch induced in her. 'We've all been busy,' she managed to say, her voice cracking.

He glanced at her and then said, 'It's been going well, don't you think?'

'Very well. It promises to be a good film.' Jennie flushed as she noted the presumption her tone implied, but Derek only chuckled.

They pulled up in front of the hotel. 'Come to my room when you're ready and we can have a quick drink before setting off. About twenty minutes?'

Jennie nodded. Refusing now to let herself think, she went into her room, took off her clothes and took a brisk shower. Then she pulled out the frothy lace skirt and top Daniela had encouraged her to buy. She hadn't worn it yet, had been saving it for goodness knows what reason. As she put it on now she saw how the white accented the glow of her skin and the scalloped edges of the blouse set off the soft haze of her dark hair. She dabbed on some lipstick and eyeshadow and stood back from the mirror taking in the effect. Not bad, she thought, looking at herself critically. Perhaps she could now provide the competition Daniela had said she wanted what seemed like a decade ago in London. She caught herself contradicting her own resolve of just a few days before and could only shrug at her own inconsistency.

She walked slowly on her high-heeled sandals towards Derek's room, feeling the swish of the skirt around her bare legs, and knocked at the door. He was holding the telephone in one hand as he opened it and gestured for Jennie to come in. She hesitated. He had obviously only had time to don his trousers before the telephone rang. His chest was bare, deeply golden against the creamy white of his trousers. He gestured to her again and Jennie crossed the threshold, her heart beating too quickly for comfort. She sat down, crossing one smooth leg over another, and flicked through a magazine she saw lying on the table. Anything to keep her eyes away from him.

It was almost an unnecessary gesture, for she could feel him intensely as he towered behind her. He ran a finger along her back where her skin met her blouse and down the line of her bare arm. Jennie shivered and made to move, but his hand on her shoulder kept her in place. At last he put the phone down.

'Sorry about that,' he came round to face her. 'It was the call from Palermo I'd been waiting for.' Gold flecks suddenly flickered in the blue of his eyes, giving him the look of some predatory animal, a tiger, Jennie thought. But he smiled at her warmly.

'You look wonderful, like some nut-brown maiden about to dance round the maypole.' Jennie's tan hid the flush his gaze brought to her cheeks, and she fidgeted uncomfortably.

'I'll be ready in a minute,' he said, reaching for the silky shirt which lay on the bed. She watched his fingers quickly doing up buttons, his agile movements as he flung a matching jacket over his shoulder. 'Right, I'm ready,' he said, passing a hand through the rough tangle of burnished hair. 'But I'd promised you a drink . . . care for one now, or later?'

'Later.' She rose and preceded him through the door he held open for her. She felt his eyes on her back with the same intensity she remembered from that day back in the London studios when she had first become aware of him-it seemed an eternity ago.

A silence developed between them as they drove to Palermo. For Jennie, it was a silence so full of unspoken thoughts that the air felt thick, so thick that her breath seemed to come with difficulty. As she flashed secret glances at Derek from beneath lowered lids, took in the shape of his hands on the wheel, the mobility of his profile, she realised that his movements gave her pleasure, almost the kind of pleasure she experienced in front of a favourite sculpting. Perhaps, she hastened to affirm to herself, that was all it was, just a visual delight.

The car wove its way through Palermo's busy streets and pulled up short at a red light. Derek flashed a look at her, as if he had read her thoughts.

'You're doing a little retreat into yourself away from me, aren't you?'

'There isn't so very far to retreat,' Jennie retorted more coldly than she had intended.

'So that's the kind of evening it's going to be,' he sighed impatiently. 'I thought we'd got beyond that childishness.'

The set of his jaw was suddenly harsh as he jerked the car
away from the light. 'Perhaps you'd like a little time on
your own before we have dinner. I could drop you off at
the cathedral while I tend to some business. It might put
you in a better frame of mind.'

'If that's what you'd prefer,' she replied, her voice cool.

He set her down in front of the cathedral and she
nodded stiffly to his brusque, 'Pick you up in about forty
minutes.'

It was only when the car had pulled away and she had
taken a deep breath that Jennie looked around her. An
audible gasp escaped her lips. Never had she seen a cathedral like this. Her eyes roamed over the many spires, the
intricate decoration, and rested on the august portals.
Jennie laughed. The odd mixture of styles was somehow
magnificently playful: lofty solemn Norman shapes set
against riotous Moorish motifs. She strode through the
doors swinging her bag as if she had suddenly been filled
with fresh energy. Inside she was greeted by the sparkle of
Byzanto-Moorish mosaics, each richer in colour than the
last. She lost herself happily in their pattern of whorls,
remembering to look at her watch only when these gave
way to the more sombre tombs of Sicilian kings. She
realised her time was up. Indeed, she was already late.
She hurried out into the *piazza*, now dusky in the receding
light, yet filled with the chatter of numerous strollers. She
spotted Derek's car waiting for her in the arranged spot
and ran towards it, almost bumping into a gaunt old man
playing a Jew's harp. Its dull twang echoed round her.

Suddenly she felt a staying hand on her shoulder, and a
chill ran through her as she veered round. The face that
confronted her made her mouth drop in amazement.

'Hello, Jennie. Fancy bumping into you here!'

She looked up into Max's bespectacled eyes and shuddered away from the hand on her shoulder.

'What an extraordinary coincidence!' He examined her
with evident curiosity. 'I've been watching you in the

cathedral and only now decided it couldn't be anyone else. You look wonderful—quite a new woman.'

He seemed to be leering at her from beneath his lank brown hair, and Jennie moved a few steps back as she uttered a low, 'Hello, Max.'

'Yes, quite a new woman,' his eyes roved over her. 'I gather someone has made you into one.' He muttered the words almost inaudibly.

Jennie stopped herself from raising a hand to slap him hard. He reached forward to take her arm and she drew abruptly away from him. His touch filled her with the nightmarish memory of the revulsion and then the pain he had once aroused in her.

Max seemed not to notice. 'Come on, let me buy you a drink and we can catch up on each other's lives.'

'Not now, Max, I'm meeting someone,' Jennie blurted out, a note of uncontrollable fear in her voice.

He seemed about to protest when a tall bronzed figure strode between them.

'Made a new friend, Jennie?' Derek's tone carried a veiled challenge. Jennie wasn't quite sure whether it was directed at her or at Max.

Max chuckled, 'Hardly a new friend, am I, Jennie?' The intimacy his words implied made her squirm.

'Hardly an old one either,' she darted back at him, and without thinking, took hold of Derek's arm.

'I wouldn't agree to that.' Max tried to catch her eye, then he turned to Derek. 'I was just suggesting to Jennie that we have a drink together. It's such a strange coincidence meeting here after all this time.'

Derek looked at Jennie expectantly, but she said nothing.

'You might introduce me to your friend, Jennie, then perhaps we can *all* have a drink together.'

Jennie made perfunctory introductions, wishing all the time that Max would vanish. She watched the two men shaking hands. Max seemed altogether dwarfed into insignificance by Derek's presence, somehow shrunken.

And yet the proportions he had taken on in her mind had been so great! Derek ushered them towards a nearby café, while Max explained that he was in Palermo for the Easter term break with a group of art students.

'And what are you doing here, Jennie? Holidaying with Derek?' he queried.

'Working on a film,' she answered tersely as they sat down at an outdoor table.

Derek gave her a quick glance. Her tone, obviously too hostile, had surprised him. But Jennie felt she could do nothing about it. She knew she was barely under control, could feel her skin growing clammy at the sheer proximity of Max. All the anxieties she thought she had put aside were taking over, again. And what if Derek should find out about her and Max? She huddled into her chair, trying to make herself small.

Max's voice took on a patronising note. 'I knew you wouldn't stick the course, Jennie. It's a hard life being a painter. Much nicer working in films.' His voice carried a sneer.

Derek laughed throatily, somehow obliterating Max altogether. 'I can see you've never worked anywhere close to film. And as for Jennie's painting, I can assure you, it goes on, despite all her other work.' Derek smiled warmly at her.

'I guess Jennie hasn't told you she was once a student of mine.' Max seemed to be taking a different tack now, as if his association with Jennie was a mark of success.

'Only very briefly,' Jennie intervened. She thought she saw Derek wink at her almost imperceptibly, and looked into his strong face with relief. If only he could read her mind now and get them away from Max as soon as possible! But before she knew it, Max had engaged Derek in what seemed an interminable discussion of mosaics. It was evident that Max was striving to score intellectual points. As the stream of words poured from his thin lips, he kept glancing at Jennie to gauge the success of his performance. She shivered again at the sight of those lips and felt the whole ordeal of the past rising in her like nausea, stopping her breath.

Derek's eyes caught hers. His words had been fewer than Max's, but through the haze of her emotions Jennie had read on Max's face the impact Derek's statements carried. He effortlessly demanded respect, engendered confidence. Max, she suddenly realised, seemed childishly vain by comparison.

Now Derek pulled his chair back from the table and signalled to the waiter. 'I'm afraid we'll really have to go if we're not to be late.'

Max seemed to recognise that he had been dismissed. He turned to Jennie. 'I'll give you a ring at your hotel, shall I, Jennie? It really is time we got to know each other again.'

Jennie shrugged, 'I'm very busy.'

'I'm sure the powers that be will give you a break to see an old friend.' Max's tone was insinuating as he looked from Derek to Jennie. 'Where did you say you were staying?'

'I don't believe I did,' Jennie said coldly.

There was an uncomfortable pause.

Derek intervened. 'We're *all*,' he emphasised the word, 'staying in Cefalu.' He shook Max's proffered hand with remote politeness and led Jennie off towards the car.

He only spoke again when they were well away from the café. 'What was all that about?' he drawled. 'The air was so thick, I could have cut it with a knife.'

Jennie felt too drained to reply.

'An old beau of yours, I gather,' Derek persisted. 'Or perhaps not so old, given the effect he seems to have on you.' He stopped the car at the side of a tree-lined street and placing a finger under her chin urged her to face him. 'Is he the one who hurt you, Jennie?' He stroked her hair and waited for her to answer.

Jennie drew away. Derek's touch seared her, served to confuse her even further. She was shocked by the pain Max's presence had woken in her. In the last few weeks she had felt that somehow he was well in the past, his memory put to rest, that she could begin to live a little more openly. And now the hurt of it all engulfed her again. She could feel the defensive wall forming once more.

'He obviously still has a hold on you.' Derek sounded irritated now, impatient, as he waited for her to speak.

'And why should it matter to you?' The words tumbled out, before Jennie realised.

Derek met her eyes for a long moment. He seemed to be reflecting. 'Obviously it does,' he said softly. Then he flashed her a half-humorous look and his face took on a defiant expression. 'You might at least pretend that you're a little pleased to be with me. I've worked hard to arrange some time to take you out for this thank-you dinner— very hard. So not one further thought about this wretched past of yours.' He fixed her with a mockingly hypnotic glare. 'Just concentrate on me, oh, mysterious and haunted lady.'

Jennie took in Derek's concentrated stare and the invisible watch he swung in front of her eyes like some silent-movie hypnotist. He was so melodramatically comical that she burst out laughing, knowing full well that it was a choice between that or tears.

'That's better,' he said, touching her mouth with light lips. 'And now, Miss Lewis, you must focus all your attention on me and be pleasant. *That* is an order.'

Jennie moved her hands to her mouth and in mime painted a wide smile on her face. 'There, I think my pleasant mask is firmly in place. If you're very nice, it may just hold for a few hours.'

'Good,' he grinned, his eyes playful, 'because I've something special in store for you.' He gave her a large mocking wink as he opened the car door for her and led her out to the edge of a little square where a row of extravagantly-painted carts, each with its own well-groomed horse, waited. He helped her up into one and climbed in beside her, giving the driver instructions. The horse ambled off, pulling the cart lightly behind him.

'Not quite ideal in traffic fumes, these *carrozzi*, but we can pretend,' Derek smiled at her warmly. 'Imagine a moonlit night in nineteenth century Palermo. Ladies lift their long dresses above seductive ankles to protect themselves from muddy streets, while stiffly honourable gentlemen keep their eyes focussed on mud to catch an occasional glimpse of ankle.'

Jennie laughed. 'All we need is a darkly clad chaperone keeping guard over us.'

'And while we're pretending,' he wound his arm around her bare shoulders and drew her close, 'two young lovers have escaped the steely eyes of the duenna and are off on a nocturnal tryst. They can't keep their hands off each other,' he wound his arm more firmly round her waist, 'or their lips.' He lifted her face to his and pressed his mouth mellowly to hers.

Jennie felt a warm flame leap inside her, and her lips melted to his.

'As long as we're just pretending,' she emphasised, her eyes bright when he released her at last.

'Yes, just pretending.' He drew her to him again, the pressure of his lips more urgent now.

Only when the horse's trot seemed to have died away completely, to be replaced by the raucous voice of the driver, did Jennie surface from his embrace, reluctant to leave a warmth which seemed to have burnt away all memory. Derek's smouldering eyes searched hers briefly before he turned to pay the driver.

They stepped down into a cypress-lined *piazza* and he took her arm to lead her down a narrow but brightly-lit street. Pausing before a restaurant door, he bowed deeply, 'After you, *mia donna*.'

Jennie smiled and preceded him into the softly-lit restaurant. After Derek had exchanged a few words with the maître d'hotel, they were guided through tall glass doors into a little garden fragrant with magnolia. Bright purple blooms clothed whitewashed walls.

'It's charming,' Jennie breathed, sitting down happily into an ornate cane chair.

'Not half so charming as you . . . when you're pretending,' Derek gave her a mocking glance.

'Flattery will get you just about anywhere at the moment,' she bantered back.

'I'll remember that,' he smiled at her obvious good humour, and passed her a menu.

They ate—lightly scented bouillabaisse, a fish Jennie didn't recognise, poached in wine and herbs, a rich creamy *zabaglione*. Perhaps it was the wine, but she suddenly found herself talking about her childhood in response to Derek's questions. His curiosity about her seemed endless. She told him the little she remembered about her real father, an engineering draughtsman.

'So that's where you get your graphic eye from,' he intervened.

'Don't know. Perhaps.' Jennie smiled and suddenly remembered how as a young child she had treasured the delicate drawings of flowers her father had done for her. They had vanished when she was moved to her aunt's.

'It must have been difficult being thrust into your aunt and uncle's child-filled household, after being your mum's only daughter,' Derek looked at her affectionately. 'Why don't you just come right out and admit you hated it, instead of insisting how kind everyone was to you?'

'They *were* kind,' Jennie stressed and then grimaced, 'But you're right, I hated it. I felt like a total misfit.'

'And that's why you insist on being such a solitary now,' he reached for her hand and held it gently, 'in case anyone who gets to know you as you are makes you feel like a misfit again. All that don't-touch-me armour. It's not unbecoming,' he looked at her reflectively, 'but it can't make you very happy.'

Jennie felt tears stinging her eyes and fought them back. Derek sounded as if he genuinely cared.

'I imagine that Max fellow has contributed to all that as well, hasn't he?'

Jennie drew her hand away. 'I guess he has——' her voice trailed off and she shied away from Derek's pressing glance. 'But that's quite enough about me, Mr Writer-Detective.' She forced her voice to be casual, rose and excused herself from the table.

Derek's eyes searched her face. 'We really aren't all the same, you know,' he said quietly as she moved away.

Jennie couldn't quite face a conversation about Max now. That she knew. Her nerves were too exposed. And it would be too shaming, would leave her too vulnerable. Derek, she realised, was moving dangerously close.

He seems to see right through me at times, she told her image framed in the powder room mirror. More clearly than I see myself.

And what if he came even closer and she found herself suffering from the same revulsion Max had engendered in her? No, she told her image decidedly. No, Max's kisses had never been like that. Either that, or the Sicilian sun, with considerable help from Derek, had changed her beyond recognition. She trembled as she thought of the sensations Derek's touch evoked in her, the feelings he stirred in her.

No, it was far more likely that Derek, having satisfied his curiosity about her, would simply grow bored, uninterested. She might be in love with him—her image gasped as she acknowledged it so directly—but why should he return that love? And on top of it all, there was the whole matter of Daniela: beautiful, clever Daniela.

Jennie shuddered. She would have to be on her guard, if she wanted to avoid the pain of ultimate rejection. She couldn't live through all that again. Forcing herself to stand tall, she steeled herself against Derek's charms and walked back towards the garden table.

It was almost as if her thoughts had dictated what was to come. Two figures stood by Derek's side. Jennie paused, her heart sinking. There was Daniela, dazzling in a fuchsia sheath, her arm on Derek's shoulder. Next to her, a plump white-suited man Jennie didn't recognise. Jennie walked slowly towards them and as Daniela saw her, the actress's eyes gleamed anger. Jennie could see her face shaping itself into a wide artificial smile.

'So that's who you've run off with,' she shook her head as if in disbelief. 'Oh, these men! And here I told Enrico that you had important business in Palermo, and possibly, just possibly, if you finished early, we might find you in this restaurant.'

Derek's eyes grew black with controlled anger, but his voice remained calm. 'Jennie, this is Enrico Palandri, one of the producers of our film. I've asked Daniela and him to join us, but I'm afraid he doesn't speak much English.'

'Oh, Jennie's Italian must be excellent by now. She learns so quickly.' Daniela's voice was tart, full of implied meaning as she looked Jennie up and down. 'The outfit I chose for you looks wonderfully well, *è vero*, Derek?'

Jennie shook the plump man's hand and sat quietly in her corner. The conversation proceeded in Italian and after a few minutes she gave up trying to follow the rapid exchange.

She drank her coffee, aware that Derek seemed to have altogether forgotten her presence; aware too of Daniela's hand placed comfortably on his cream-suited arm, her fingers playing carelessly with the fabric. Only once did the actress look directly at Jennie and then her eyes seemed to flash a clear 'hands off' signal. Gone was any of the warmth she had previously scattered in Jennie's direction.

Derek seemed immune to the silent war between the two women, and by the time Jennie had finished her coffee, her mind was made up. She would leave them, she obviously had no place here. She rose and with terse politeness said, 'If you'll excuse me, I'll go for a stroll. You evidently have important business to attend to.' She gave Derek a scathing glance, but he seemed oblivious to her gesture and the others only nodded cursorily.

She left the restaurant, kept the tears away from her eyes and idled randomly along the narrow street. She realised that her irritation was selfishly childish, but under it lay a deeper sense of hopelessness. It was clear that Derek was mildly interested in her. Probably she should feel flattered. But she didn't. She felt dismally hurt, angry at the way he kowtowed to Daniela's every move, and worse, somehow debased at the way he was playing with her. She swallowed thickly, and tried to push her thoughts away by looking unseeingly into shop windows.

She wandered into a small, dark *piazza*, letting her feet carry her where they would. The sound of echoing footsteps on cobblestones behind her made her turn in fear as she realised that she was quite alone in the small square. Suddenly a hand grabbed for her shoulder bag. She struggled, briefly saw the glint of yellow eyes in a dark face. The last thing she remembered was a hand pushing her hard as she screamed and toppled over on the pavement.

CHAPTER EIGHT

THE next thing Jennie knew she was lying on a bed, her head aching painfully. She stretched her hands and could feel stiff sheets. When she opened her eyes, she made out the anaesthetic white, murky green and chrome of what was undeniably a hospital room. She raised her head slowly, groaning a little at its leaden weight. A form got up from a chair in the grey light of the room. Derek was before her, his face gaunt with tiredness.

'Good morning,' he tried a smile. 'How do you feel?'

'Headachy,' Jennie grimaced. 'What happened? How did I get here?'

'Every day in Palermo's recent history, a number of people are mugged.' Derek sounded as if he were quoting by rote. 'The city proliferates in pickpockets. According to the most recent census . . .' his voice trailed off. 'Any Baedeker will warn you not to wander the streets alone at night, Jennie.' His voice was gruff.

'I'm sorry,' he took her hand gently, 'it's my fault. I took a little too long to say goodbye to Enrico and Daniela before coming after you. I thought you'd be waiting outside, but there was no sign of you, so I looked round trying to think which way you'd gone. Then I heard a scream and came running. I found you lying by the kerb. You must have hit your head on it, rather hard from the look of things.'

Jennie felt her head and a small groan twisted her smile. 'I've given birth to an egg, it seems.'

'As long as it's no more than that.' Derek's eyes were heavy with concern. 'They'll do some X-rays later this morning. Oh, Jennie, I am sorry.' Self-criticism hardened his voice.

Jennie squeezed the hand enveloping hers. 'You're not to blame. I'm an idiot, I seem to get into constant trouble here.'

She took in his crumpled trousers, the shadow of beard on his strong jaw, as he paced the room.

'And you've been sitting here all night?'

He looked at her quizzically. 'I thought you might like to see a familiar face when you woke up.'

'I'm very, very pleased that you're here——' her voice broke as she said it and met his eyes.

He sat down on the bed and fingered the rim of her hospital nightshirt. Jennie felt tears looming at the back of her eyes and kept them back with an effort. She gave him a tremulous smile.

He took it in. 'It's all right now. Just rest and with luck we'll have you out of here by this afternoon.'

She nodded and then looked down at herself. 'I see they've managed to undress me.' She gave him a questioning look.

'They,' he stressed, 'have. Your clothes are in that closet, a little the worse for wear, I'm afraid. I'll bring you some fresh ones when I come back this afternoon.'

'Do you have to go then?' she asked, panic suddenly mounting in her. She felt very small and alone.

'I'm sorry, love, I'm afraid I do.' He looked at her entreatingly and standing up, paced away from her. 'Damn,' he muttered under his breath, then turned towards her. 'Enrico is coming on location today and I said I would see him.'

An image of Enrico and Daniela on the previous evening sprang into Jennie's mind and she selfishly felt unable to affirm the importance of his going. Her head suddenly throbbed, and she lay back into the pillows. Derek was at her side instantly, his face suffused with tenderness.

'Does it hurt a great deal?'

'A little,' she acknowledged. And then, feeling guilt at the trouble she was so unnecessarily causing him, she added, 'But I'll be all right. Don't worry,' she smiled, putting all the assurance she could into it. 'I'll be perfectly all right.' He squeezed her hand just as a Sister, clad in bristling white, opened the door with a tray.

'*Buon giorno!*' she called with professional cheer and then babbled away in a swift Italian Jennie understood nothing of. But the tray she placed before her showed hot coffee and rolls, and when her pillows were propped and fluffed, she gratefully sipped the hot liquid. She passed Derek her cup and he drank a mouthful before giving her a light kiss.

'I'll be back as soon as I can,' he said quietly, and left her to the Sister's cheerful gabble.

Jennie drank her coffee, nibbled a little of the rolls and then sank into the pillows, 'Love,' he had said to her, she remembered, as she closed her eyes and sank into a light sleep.

She woke to the sound of the door opening. A nurse entered carrying a bundle of magazines and papers. '*Il signore*,' she gestured with her hands to denote height.

'*Grazie*,' Jennie said in her best accent, and leafed through the bundle. Derek had brought her everything imaginable from *The Times* to *Newsweek*. From somewhere in the mass of papers, an envelope emerged with her name on it. Jennie tore it open. 'Rest,' it said in bold letters, 'I'll see you very soon.'

Jennie felt strangely blessed. A smile hovered over her lips as she flicked through the bundle. She read here and there as items caught her interest. In one of the papers she happened to see a diary piece about their film. Derek and Matthew were mentioned in glowing terms. Thrilled, she tore it out and put it on the small night table. Just then a doctor walked into the room.

'*E l'inglesa*,' she heard the nurse say.

The doctor examined her somewhat brusquely, mumbling about silly tourists beneath his breath, and ushered her off towards the X-ray room.

Jennie noticed that most of the wards were crammed with beds and wondered at how she had managed to be in her own room. Derek, she suddenly thought. No wonder the doctor had mistaken her for some wealthy tourist!

The X-ray over, she padded back to her room and dropped gratefully down on the bed.

When she woke some time later, it took her a moment to remember her whereabouts. The sun was already low in the sky. She glanced at her watch: four o'clock, she had almost slept the day through. She moved her head gingerly, relieved to feel the painful throbbing had subsided a little. She wished Derek would arrive.

The sound of the door opening made her look up expectantly, and a sharp stab pierced through her. Max stood in the doorway.

He looked down at her with an inappropriate grin.

'Poor Jennie,' he shook his head. 'The hotel told me you'd had an "accident". It seems your new man isn't taking care of you too well.' He gloated over her. 'Perhaps you should have come with me yesterday after all.'

Jennie searched for words with which she could lunge out at him, cut him to the quick. But only a steely, 'Leave me alone, Max,' came to her lips. It had an oddly definitive ring to it. Its very sound began to give her strength.

But Max smiled smugly. 'I have, for quite a long time, if you remember. But it seems you might be ready for me now.' He touched her arm with a moist hand and removing his glasses, looked her over with a clinical gaze.

A shrill laugh suddenly escaped Jennie's lips. 'I'll never be ready for you Max. Never!' Her smouldering hatred, the desire for revenge she had long kept hidden even from herself, had all at once transformed itself into contempt. Max seemed small, devoid of the power he had long had over her, not particularly worthy of the place he had taken in her reflections.

'It's simple, Max,' she said, her tone crisp. 'Can't you see I don't care for you any more? It must have been a childish infatuation, no more than that. Hardly surprising, given the attention you paid me, the power you had over a mere student.'

It was out, and as she said it, she was struck by the truth of her words.

But Max was not so easily to be dismissed. An insinuating grin spread over his face. 'I'm the first to be pleased that you're no longer a child.' Before Jennie could move away, he plunged his lips down on hers.

'Excuse me if I'm intruding,' a deep voice burst in upon them.

Jennie pulled away from Max's unwanted kiss, feeling the flush rising to her face. Derek's eyes were dark with rage, while Max looked disgustingly pleased with himself, like a small boy who had just stolen an exceptionally tasty biscuit.

'I've brought you your things, Jennie.' Derek towered over her and all but threw her overnight bag down on the floor. Then he turned away and seemed to be on the point of leaving.

Jennie found her voice. 'Max was just saying goodbye,' she announced emphatically. 'Goodbye, Max,' her words ordered him away.

Max paused, seemed about to protest and then changed his mind. He glanced selfconsciously at his watch. 'Yes, I really must be getting back to my students. See you soon, Jennie. Very soon.' He bent again to kiss her and then stretched out his hand to Derek, who seemed not to notice. Max shrugged and moved towards the door, only looking back to give Jennie a slow, deliberate wink.

Conceited fool, Jennie thought to herself; but her mind was already with Derek. He looked more tired than Jennie remembered, his face pale beneath the tan, his shoulders hunched with repressed anger.

'The nurse tells me you can go now,' he said, his voice rigidly formal. 'I'll wait outside while you dress. Unless you'd rather have Max take you back?' He kept his eyes fixed on a space somewhere above her head.

Jennie shook her head. Her heart sank at Derek's tone. The closeness of the morning was shattered. She watched Derek's broad back receding through the door and tears burned her eyelids. It would be too late to recapture his tenderness now. He must think she had lied to him about Max being merely a forgotten figure from the past. And once they were back with the others, once Daniela was present, Derek's attention would inevitably focus elsewhere. Now that she had done his mural for him and he had thanked her properly, what further need was there for contact?

Jennie sighed deeply and then with something like relief, got out of bed and reached for her bag. She noted that it contained far more than she needed, and having rummaged through her clothes, she pulled on a pair of jeans and a black tee-shirt with deliberate movements. Then she took a long breath and tried a smile. A new mood seemed to be overtaking her. To her surprise, she felt strangely calm.

Perhaps it's better this way, she thought to herself. She would at last be her own woman again. Max's memory, the pain he had caused her seemed finally to have been put to rest by his reappearance as a more than ordinary mortal. And Derek—well, since he couldn't love her, he could only end by hurting her. Jennie smiled a wry smile and squared her shoulders. So that was that! She was better off without men anyway. They had never done her any good.

Jennie pulled her long legs into Derek's car and sat as far away from him as possible. He seemed sullen, impatient, closed to her. He didn't ask her how she felt, simply moved

the car fitfully through congested streets. She noticed that
he didn't take the turning marked Cefalu.

'Haven't you missed our road?' she broke the silence.

He started at the sound of her voice, as if he had forgotten her presence. Then he said gruffly, 'We're not
going to Cefalu.'

'Can I ask where we are going, then?'

'You'll see.' He glanced at her briefly and jammed his
foot on the accelerator so that the car leapt forward with
dizzying speed.

Jennie forced all questions away from her tongue and
made herself relax into the car's upholstery. They were
climbing past grey-green olive groves now, up into
rounded hills which seemed eternal in their solidity. The
air had an eerie hush in the setting sunlight and for no
explicable reason Jennie felt sure that they were close to
hidden necropoli, ancient burial grounds enclosed by
wind-shaped trees. When the pink glow had abruptly
given way to darkness, the lights of a mountain-top town
were suddenly upon them creating a jagged pattern
against the blue-black sky.

Derek braked to a halt in front of a white wall topped
with wrought iron fencing. 'We'll stop here.'

Jennie could make out a small sign on the side of the
wall announcing a hotel.

'For the night?' she queried.

He looked down on her. 'Yes,' he answered harshly.
'But don't worry, you'll have your own room.' His voice
sounded bored.

'I didn't expect anything else,' she replied. 'But you do
realise I haven't penny or passport on me?'

He shrugged, 'Greater problems have been sur-
mounted.'

He took her bag out of the car and she noticed that he
had his own smaller one with him. Had it all been
planned? Jennie was puzzled. She followed him into the
small hotel, its tiled floors colourful with Arabic patterns

and sparkling with cleanliness. While he fulfilled reception formalities, she glanced round the immaculate lobby. He returned quickly and handed her a key.

'I'm going to have dinner on the terrace in a little while. You can join me if you like.'

Jennie shook her head, which had begun to throb again.

'As you wish.'

They followed a suited man up a flight of stairs and along a corridor. Derek opened the door of a room, deposited her bag and ushered her in.

'I'll be next door, if you want me,' he said, his voice distant as he strode away.

Jennie switched on a bedside lamp and looked cursorily around the room before she threw herself down on the wide bed. Derek's behaviour was a mystery. Why bring her here when he was obviously totally uninterested in her presence? She thought of his coldness, his distraction and uncustomary rudeness. She was now totally dependent on him, quite oblivious of her whereabouts and penniless to boot. A knot of reaction mixed with regret formed in her stomach. That very morning he had looked on her with such tenderness that she had almost thought . . . but no, she refused to pursue that track.

She got up and looked in her bag to see if it held a nightdress. It did, and she wondered briefly if Derek had packed for her. She took off her clothes slowly, noticed a door and opened it to find a small tidy bathroom. She ran a bath and lay down in its soothing depths, trying to still the beating in her head. When the hot water had cooled perceptibly around her, she got up, towelled herself dry and slipped into the pale cotton nightdress. Its folds fell loosely round her as she walked towards the window of the small room. Next to it she noticed a glass door which led out on to a tiny terrace. She opened it and stepped out. The air was chill and Jennie thought she detected a scent of pines. She breathed in the sharp fragrance deeply and then, feeling cold, went back to the bed and cuddled in its softness. Sleep seemed far away and she simply reclined there, unable to stop the many images of the last few days from pervading her mind. Foremost among them was one of Max and Derek sitting side by side in the café. She smiled to herself. If nothing else, Derek had certainly cured her of Max.

A knock at the door roused her from her thoughts.

'Come in!' she called.

The door opened on to a white-shirted waiter carrying a silver tray. Behind him came Derek.

'I thought you might like a little food, after all,' he said.

Jennie sat up. The smell of the food made her realise she was very hungry. 'Oh, yes, please!'

Derek grinned. 'I'm glad to see the stint in hospital hasn't ruined your appetite.' He poured her a glass of wine. 'Drink this, it will do you good.' He looked at her lazily. 'Mind if I keep you company for a while?'

Jennie gestured towards the chair by her bedside. She could feel his eyes on her as she focussed her attention on the tray in front of her.

'Does your head still hurt?' he asked gently.

'A little,' she conceded, meeting his eyes.

His face was level with hers now and she noticed the dark shadows under his eyes, the tautness of his mouth. Her eyes travelled downwards to his tensed shoulders and her heart went out to him in all his pent-up masculinity.

'You look worse than I do,' she said softly.

'It's been a rough day, with one thing and another,' he took a large sip from his wine glass, 'but I'm glad that that Max creature has left you capable of noticing.'

Jennie winced at his words and at the sight of the sardonic gleam in his eyes.

He brought out a packet of cigarettes from his pocket. 'May I?'

She nodded.

He lit up taking a long slow puff and breathing the smoke out thickly.

'Did I snap at you before?'

Jennie found herself giggling. 'Yes, you certainly did.'

'I guess I should apologise,' he stubbed out his cigarette. 'I was in a foul temper. And that Max of yours didn't help. I'm a little more human now.' He suddenly smiled the golden intimate smile which sent tremors through her.

'I'll let you sleep now. See you in the morning.' He blew her a kiss and left the room.

Jennie turned over on her side, her heart full of un-expressed emotion. How she would have loved to run her fingers through his hair, smooth that tensed brow. But no, she stopped the flood of emotions which suddenly filled her. Better to keep a distance, she reminded herself, and then smiled. A friendly distance.

No sooner had Jennie opened her eyes that next morning than a knock sounded on the door, followed by the appearance of a young girl bearing a breakfast tray. She deposited it on the small table, flashed Jennie a smile and disappeared. Shafts of sunlight streaming through the wooden shutters dispelled Jennie's semi-consciousness and reminded her of where she was. She rubbed her eyes, watched the strips of gold playing over the room and stretched languidly before rising to examine the breakfast tray. She drank some coffee, nibbled at the rolls, then lazily went to run a bath.

Derek's voice penetrated her reverie as she lay in the foaming water.

'Are you ready?'

'Give me fifteen minutes!' she called back, and rose to dress.

As she looked in the small dressing-table mirror, she tried to work out what day of the week it was. Time, of which she was usually so aware, seemed to evade her in the Sicilian sun. Now she had lost track again. Was it Saturday or Sunday? She shrugged. She was at Derek's mercy whatever the case. Dark pockets of blue circled her eyes and made them stand out strangely in her brown face. She donned her sunglasses, threw her few possessions into the bag and shut the door of the room quietly behind her.

Derek was waiting in the flower-strewn front garden. His long legs stretched in front of him, he was leaning against a railing and seemed to be lost in thought, unaware of her until she was upon him. Even then it seemed to take him some time to remember who she was. It made her angry.

'Hello,' he said at last. 'Sleep well?'

'Like a lost soul.'

He arched an eyebrow. 'Well, we're stealing a holiday today, so that should raise your spirits.'

'Do I have a choice, or do I simply do as I'm told?'

His eyes flickered over her. 'Do as you're told, woman,' he growled, his voice contradicting the sudden merriment in his face.

She bowed low. 'After you, oh, master.'

Derek flung their bags into the car and climbed in, stretching over to open Jennie's door.

He watched her swing into the seat and then bent towards her to remove her sunglasses. 'Let me look at you properly.' He gazed critically at her face. 'Hmm, not too bad for the victim of a Sicilian mugging,' he said reflectively.

'I'm thrilled to have your approval, kind master,' she glared at him.

A devilish twinkle came into his eyes. 'Come here, you little wretch!' He pulled her towards him, his grip tightening on her wrist as she resisted his pressure. Jennie struggled and then let him have his way, lying impassive in his embrace as he planted a savage kiss on her lips. He let her go, his eyes amused.

'The return of Diana. Book One, Chapter Three:

Feeling insulted by her partner's inattention, haunted by images of the past, our young heroine . . .'

Jennie raised a hand to fling a slap at his face, but he caught her wrist in mid-air. 'Uh-uh, no more of that, remember? Or I may just respond in kind?'

She looked at him aghast.

Derek chuckled, 'No, in fact it's not my way. I'd prefer to leave you stranded—penniless, passportless—on some lonely mountain top. Now that would be my idea of just punishment for ungrateful behaviour.'

Jennie reached for the car door. 'You might as well just leave me right here. I'm quite capable of making do.'

He pulled her back on the seat and looked at her sardonically.

'Of that I'm only too well aware . . . But since I'd rather not have to extricate you from any more nastiness, why don't you just stay here and listen to orders.'

'You pompous, patronising, arrogant . . .' Jennie spluttered.

He passed a long finger sensuously down her cheek. 'I know, I know—pompous, patronising, impossible bastard.' His eyes gleamed with mirth, but his voice was kind now. 'I'm joking, Jennie. Why don't you just settle back and save your energy? It's going to be a scorcher of a day.' He started the car and pulled away from the whitewashed hotel.

Jennie kept her eyes straight ahead of her, only daring to glance at him once her face was well under control. The sunlight illuminated the burnished gold of his hair, his eyes were intent now on the road. He seemed to be encased in a magnetic charge, so strong that Jennie found herself putting out a hand to touch his shoulder. It made her skin tingle and she drew away.

He glanced at her briefly and took her hand, holding it firmly in his.

'Better now?'

She nodded.

'I'm taking you to one of my favourite places, so keep your eyes open to the present, please.'

Jennie was suddenly aware of the peacock blue sky above them, the purple and pink flower-strewn hills, the town carved like stone out of the mountain top receding in the distance. She leaned back in the seat and took a deep breath.

The road wound before them, shimmering in the heat, and as the sun rose higher in the sky, a pale violet haze seemed to swim over everything. Soon, almost as if they had crossed an invisible line, the landscape began to change. Wild flowers gave way to golden wheatfields iridescent in the sun. The air took on a dusty dryness as if it were filled with wisps of straw. In a little valley, where Jennie thought she made out the strange shape of a carob tree, Derek pulled up at a petrol station.

'Drink?' he offered.

'Yes, please.' Jennie felt a midsummer thirst parching her tongue.

They walked to a small bar at the side of the station and he ordered two tall glasses of a white icy liquid. Jennie sipped in a sugary sweetness, and grimaced.

'See if you can guess what it is.'

She shook her head. 'Milk, perhaps honey?'

He laughed, 'And almond juice.'

She drained her glass and the waiter brought another. Watching Derek, tall, broad-shouldered, leaning lazily against the counter, his face smiling as he exchanged words with the waiter, a strange dreaminess overtook her. Words of a biblical ring came to her mind, she had no idea from where. 'When the sons of gods came down to the daughters of men.' She wanted to pinch herself to see if she were awake, but the dreaminess persisted, followed them back to the car and stayed with her as they sped along the heat-glazed road. All at once she thought she could distinguish the sea, calm as the sky in the distance, but with a still deeper shade of blue. The land had taken on a limestone configuration and on the top of a bluff stood a small cottage—perched precariously as if it were about to drop over the side at any instant-bordered by bent pines.

'So desolate!' Jennie breathed.

Derek followed the line of her gaze. 'It's a little hamlet, appropriately named Chaos. Would you like to make a detour?'

Jennie shook her head. 'I don't think so.'

'It's the birthplace of the playwright Pirandello.'

Jennie remembered the name vaguely. 'He must have had a bleak existence.'

Derek chuckled wryly. 'Produced good work out of it. But look ahead. There's Agrigento—our destination.'

Jennie thrilled at the name of this Athens of Sicily. The city lay in spirals before them, rising in limestone tiers like a dusty wedding cake baked in the noonday sun. But the wonders of the site were not matched by the city itself. It was quite unlike what Jennie had imagined, the streets busy with lorries, many of the buildings modern, and crammed with shops and cafés.

Derek noticed her disappointment. 'Time goes on,' he remarked, 'but if you close your eyes you can still breathe in the Attic stillness. And just wait until after lunch. No disappointments then.'

He parked on a crowded street and led her towards a restaurant. 'I'm afraid it's pasta or rice, unless you'd rather picnic?'

'Oh yes!' Jennie's eyes lit up with excitement.

She trailed after Derek as he went into numerous small shops, bought bread, salami, cheese, fruit, a bottle of wine, and then bustled her back into the car.

'Now, young lady,' he said, winking at her, 'it's off to the vale of temples.' The car curled along a modern road carved between sweeps of delicately flowering almond trees and olive groves.

Suddenly Jennie gasped. Before her were the columns

of the antique temples striding out of the terra-cotta earth
as if it had given birth to them with no help from man.
Each twist in the valley seemed to display another, bathed
in a calm untouched by time. Derek parked the car and
they followed a path, fragrant with the scent of thyme
and sage, until they came to the side of an ochre-coloured
temple which seemed strangely both grand and intimate.
Derek spread a blanket in tall grass replete with purple
and yellow flowers. When Jennie offered to help, he waved
her off in the direction of the temple.

'Have a walk round Concord. Its harmonies may soothe
you,' he said playfully.

Jennie climbed up steep slabs of steps and entered the
columned interior. She drank in the mysterious stillness of
the air, passed her hands over the sturdy columns, their
surface rough with age and thousands of small shells.
Everything—the sweep of the hills around her, the glimmer of the distant sea, the monumental columns—was
enveloped in a dreamy haze which seemed as old as time
itself. She walked slowly, intensely conscious and yet
somehow dazed. The sensation of a hand on her shoulder
did nothing to disturb her. She took the hand in hers and
continued walking, slowly, rhythmically matching the
steps at her side.

'You look like some ancient nymph—no, perhaps the
priestess of some antique cult.' His voice was low.

She smiled from some distant sense of repose.

Derek had stripped down into white shorts, his feet bare
on the stony earth. His eyes above his bronzed cheeks
were as blue as the sky. She looked at him as if he were
some emanation of the temple itself, some mortal
fathered by an impetuous antique god. Languorously,
she trailed a slender hand down his shoulder, over the
muscles of his golden chest. His eyes flickered and he
stopped her hand, taking it in his to lead her to their
grassy nook.

He had spread the centre of their blanket with napkins

on which the small heaps of tomatoes, olives and oranges shone with a blaze of colour.

'A repast for the gods,' said Jennie, suddenly shy.

'Or peasants,' he chuckled as he stooped down on the blanket. 'Have you got your bathing suit on? It's hot.'

Jennie nodded and stripped down to the white of her bikini. Derek's eyes caressed her lazily.

'These pagan sites have an overwhelming impact,' he warned sardonically as he pulled her down next to him. She flushed hotly and he laughed. 'They make one ravenously hungry!'

He broke off a piece of the large round bread and handed it to her with some slices of salami and having poured some wine into two plastic cups, served himself. They bit into their food, the sun hot overhead, the cicadas filling the air with their cacophony of sound.

'I can't imagine why Empedocles would have wanted to throw himself into Etna with all this around him,' Jennie remarked suddenly, the thought having come to her from nowhere.

'Perhaps he got tired of thinking with his blood, of the eternal strife of opposites, the war of the sexes. That's how he saw the world. You know, he thought the most perfect form in nature was a tree, because it combined both male and female.'

Jennie looked at the man at her side, this stranger so close to her who seemed to know so many things.

'But perhaps he just got tired of looking at the riot of colour which originally covered these temples. No terracotta warmth here when the temples were in use, but garish colour, painted statues. Poor Empedocles!' Derek laughed as he caught her looking at him strangely.

'How do you know all that? About Empedocles, I mean.'

He grinned, 'My parents made sure I went to university, ma'am. Read philosophy, I did. Does it show too much?'

'Hardly ever.' Jennie caught his tone and laughed.

'Good, because I'm really much more interested in you

at the moment, though God knows why, given the way you usually respond to me.'

Before Jennie could find a suitable reply, his arms were around her, his mouth strong and sweet with wine on hers. She opened to his kiss as if she had waited for it for an eternity, blissfully unaware of her previous resolve.

'That's better,' Derek murmured in her ear, covering it with kisses that sent tremors leaping through her. She let her hands glide over his back, moaning softly as she felt the texture of his skin, satin-smooth over the taut muscles, and when he found her lips again, his kiss seemed to reach her very core. He cupped her breast and fondled its delicate curve, all the while leading her fingers along his chest. With a mind of their own, they strayed to the burnished mass of his hair, traced the outlines of his brows and rugged jaw. A low groan escaped him and his firm thighs wound their way round her. As his hardness enveloped her, pressed against her, she could feel passion melting her limbs so that her blood became part of his, part of the earth, the sky, the sun, the small flowers at her feet, the stridulation of the cicadas.

'Damn!' he cursed suddenly and rolled off her, his breath uneven.

Jennie made out the sound of nearby laughter and turned to see a group of tourists climbing the steps to the temple.

'So much for Attic serenity!' His voice was light, but his eyes smouldered as he drew her into the cradle of his arms, stroking her gently. Jennie nestled against him, her skin tingling with his touch.

'Perhaps Empedocles had a point about thinking with blood,' he whispered in her ear.

'Mmm.' She raised herself on one elbow looking into his face, warm in the sun. Her voice, she felt, couldn't yet be trusted, and instead, she fingered the rough tufts of hair on his chest.

He removed her hand gently. 'Not now, or I can't

promise not to provide another spectacle for the tourists.'

He rose, pulling her up after him, and handed her her clothes.

Jennie felt her knees waver beneath her and she leaned against him as she slipped into her white sun-dress and sandals. He gathered up their things.

'Come on, let's make a vist to Juno—and the Dioscuri, mustn't forget that.'

He took her hand and led her back to the car where they dropped their bundle and then walked slowly in and around the various temples. Hot on their heads, the sun melted Jennie's thoughts. She walked as if in a trance, aware only of her body and his, their fingers coiled together in the heat. They were now treading slowly round a rather haphazard site, stone piled randomly here and there, when Jennie stopped, suddenly awake. In front of them lay a gigantic stone figure, brutal somehow in its very size. Derek laughed out loud at her expression.

'He was some kind of a man, as Marlene Dietrich might say,' he grinned.

'What?' The reference explained nothing to Jennie.

'He's called a *telamon*. Apparently there was a whole row of them, giant men over twenty-five feet tall, forming a kind of frieze, arms raised to support the temple's architrave.'

'He looks more like Gulliver in Lilliput,' a wide smile broke over Jennie's face. 'Can I step on him?'

'No one to stop you. But be careful how you treat your men,' Derek warned mischievously.

She threw him a playfully arch glance and made her way along the enormous blocks of stone which formed the giant. Her face was radiant. 'I haven't had so much fun in years,' she shouted to Derek. 'Ever . . .' her voice trailed off. She could feel his eyes on her from his distance, giving her limbs a new-found sensuality.

'That's enough of that,' he was suddenly upon her. 'I won't have you frolicking with strangers. Bad enough, your ghosts from the past. Come with me, you little wanton!' He pulled her laughing after him, and as he wound his arms round her, she slipped away and ran, happy to feel her legs moving swiftly beneath her.

He was upon her almost at once and she noticed the question in his eyes and behind it the glimmer of desire.

'You're not planning a little escape again, are you?' His voice was heavy.

'Not just yet,' Jennie smiled at him tauntingly. Looking at him, she was suddenly struck again by his rugged beauty. She lowered her eyelids, afraid that he might vanish if she gazed at him too long, and a sense of mystery pervaded her. This man, at once so intimate and so strange, these temples. She took his arm to test the reality of it all.

He passed his hand through the tangle of her hair and she winced.

'I'm sorry,' he said, his voice full of a throbbing gentleness. 'It's the egg, isn't it?'

She nodded.

'If I were a gentleman, I'd take you to a hotel now and put you to bed. Alone,' he added as an afterthought. 'But I'm not. The egg can fend for itself. You and I are going to wait for the lights to come on here. It's not to be missed.'

'The egg can certainly take care of itself,' Jennie agreed, amused. 'But as for me,' she paused provocatively, 'do you think there might be some coffee somewhere near this *telamon* of yours?'

Derek laughed. 'Your every wish, dear lady . . .'

They sat in a little bar, drinking coffee, watching the sun set over the calm of the temples. Then just as darkness fell, bells started ringing from everywhere. By a miracle of orchestration, floodlights suddenly burst on the temples, illuminating their symmetry as if for some secret ancient rite. They feasted their eyes on the sight and with no need for words rose in unison to stroll slowly round the temples.

Fireflies beat their wings in little shimmering points, while countless insects throbbed an eerie music. They found their counterpoint in Jennie's quick-beating pulse as Derek ran his fingers across the smooth skin of her neck and left a trail of sensation along her spine. She could feel love clamouring in her veins and cleaved to him as his hard lips forced her mouth to an aching surrender.

His voice was gravelly in the darkness when he released her. 'Come on.'

She followed, like a sleepwalker at the mercy of a movement not her own, her slender frame a fragile covering for the pounding of her blood, her entire being suffused with a yearning ache for the lithe night creature at her side.

She couldn't quite recollect how they had arrived there, but suddenly they were in a room with louvred doors thrown open to starlight. Derek's eyes were dark with desire as they raked over her face. His fingers on the nape of her neck beneath her heavy hair, on her throat, her breasts, cleared a path for his urgent lips. A tumult stirred in Jennie's blood, making her pulse beat wildly. She sought the sweet relief of his mouth, but its crushing weight only made her limbs molten with heaviness. With the grace of a tiger, he lifted her on to the bed and buried his glistening head in her bosom.

'So beautiful,' he breathed, his breath hot in her ear.

As she felt his firm hardness covering her, stirring secret places within her, Jennie suddenly stiffened perceptibly against him. He arched away from her and looked into her eyes enquiringly. 'What is it, Jennie?' His voice was soft.

She felt an uncontrollable sob breaking from her throat. But it was followed by no other sound.

'Don't you want me?'

She couldn't find any words with which to answer him.

A flicker of something that might have been anger passed through his eyes. Then his face registered astonishment. 'Tell me, Jennie, is it . . . is it the first time?'

She nodded, all at once overcome with a cold sadness.

'Why didn't you tell me? I thought . . . Max . . .' his voice was husky with controlled passion.

Then abruptly, before she had a chance to answer, he was far from her, looming tall over her, his face set in grimness.

'And all that high-handed business about painting male nudes, what was that? A little bit of random teasing to get your own back at these male creatures you say you so dislike?' Contempt dripped from his voice. 'Well, personally I'm not in the business of being teased or of seducing little girls who pretend to be women!'

He threw her a scathing look and before she could say anything, the door had shut behind him.

Sobs racked Jennie's slender frame, to be replaced in time only by a yawning ache in which she felt she would drown. She forced herself to get up and wash her face, pull on a nightdress, and then she huddled in her bed, trying desperately to come to terms with her desolation. A slender thread of sanity presented itself to her at last and she grasped at it: the humiliation was as much his as hers. Here she had been thinking he could see right through her! How dared he presume that she was some woman of the world out for a little sensual escapade with an attractive man? But the corollary of that line of thinking weighed heavily on her. It spelled out all too clearly that that was precisely what he too was doing: engaging in a little fling, no strings attached. The ache engulfed her again, more terrifying in its totality than anything she had felt at Max's rejection, at the recognition of what she had thought was her frigidity.

A knock at the door sent hope racing through her, but it opened to show a waiter carrying a tray. Jennie was unable to prevent a slightly hysterical giggle from rising to her throat. If nothing else, Derek was considerate about feeding her. But the laughter choked her. She poked at the food, giving it up to tumble back on the bed and let the tears cascade down her cheeks in the silence of her pillow.

She slept fitfully, waking drained and at once fully aware of everything that had passed. Glancing at her watch, she realised it was already late and the greyness of the light was due to a change of weather. She opened the shutters to a covered sky that threw a mournful light on the valley in the distance. Shuddering, she dressed quickly and went downstairs.

Derek was standing at the reception desk. She came up behind him and he turned, startled by her sudden presence. His face was tired and as their eyes met in intimacy, a pang went through her, wrenching her in half. But the moment passed as soon as it had come. His voice was politely formal.

'We'd better leave immediately. I've got to arrive in time for a meeting with Enrico.'

'I'm quite ready,' Jennie said coolly, controlling an impulse to touch him.

In the car he handed her a small package. 'I bought you a little present, a souvenir. I'm afraid I was a little unfair last night.' His eyes searched her face.

She tore open the wrapping with clumsy fingers. Inside was a small terra-cotta vase, its sunbaked earth engraved with two dancing figures, male and female. She flung it from her. 'I don't need any reminders,' she said tersely, 'reminders of the fact that you see me as a casual little diversion from your main interests.'

His face registered anger. He looked as if he were about to shake her and only the greatest of self-control prevented him.

'Suit yourself.' His voice was harsh.

They drove silently, swiftly, as if Derek's urge to get back propelled the car. When they reached the mountains, a fog filled with cold raindrops descended and he stopped to put up the car's hood.

'Weather to suit our mood,' he said grimly.

Headway was slow now, and Jennie could feel Derek's barely contained rage enveloping her. She sat stiffly, her head beginning to throb with tension.

When they finally arrived back at the hotel, his glance rested on her only for a moment as he passed her her bag before striding off with an almost inaudible, 'Take care of yourself.'

Jennie went to the reception desk to get her key, and with a wide smile, the assistant handed her her stolen bag.

She chuckled wryly to herself at the small mercies the day had brought. Then she walked slowly to her room, threw herself on her bed and gazed listlessly at the ceiling.

CHAPTER NINE

AT Kathy's insistence, Jennie went down to dinner that evening. Her pallor, her low spirits were luckily explained by the mugging, and Kathy's solicitousness helped to make the meal pass. They were joined by Piero, whose concern for Jennie voiced itself in criticism of conditions in Sicily and the need to change them. His passionate analysis, the care he showered on her, almost made her forget her despondency. He had really became something of a friend. It was only when she saw Derek entering the dining room with Matthew, Enrico and Daniela that her sense of desolation came flooding back. She excused herself, pleading fatigue and the need to rest before tomorrow morning's early start.

The next morning rose bright and clear in total contradiction to Jennie's mood.

'Oh, do cheer up, Jennie,' Kathy pleaded with her as they dressed. 'We're off to a new location today and I can't wait to see more sights.'

Jennie forced a smile, making sure it stayed on her face to please Kathy. They tumbled into the bus, but Jennie saw nothing of the scenery on the way and when they emerged in a little lowland hamlet surrounded by olive groves terraced in lava black rock, she was barely aware of the eerie beauty of the scene. More dark faces greeted her, this time in a somewhat more comfortable home; more children; more coffee. She set out her things and waited for Daniela and the other actors to arrive.

But when Daniela did, Jennie was unprepared for the shock of the encounter.

'Ah, you're back, are you? I thought I might be spared

your incompetence for another few days,' she said vehemently as she flounced into a chair.

Jennie bristled, but she controlled an angry retort,
simply motioning for Daniela to move in front of a mirror.
Kathy looked on, worried. Jennie slipped a plastic cap
over Daniela's hair.

'I'm afraid it's back to the old matron today, Daniela.'
Jennie couldn't keep a note of irony out of her voice.

Daniela gave her a scathing glance, 'If you want to
play competitive games, my little girl, be very careful. I
promise you I'll win. I'll win *him*.' Her green eyes flashed
warning at Jennie, but then she said nothing more. It was
only after Jennie had finished making her up and she
looked at herself in the mirror that Daniela let her temper
fly. Jennie stood back, shocked by its vehemence.

'*No, è impossibile!*' Daniela rose out of her chair sending
it toppling behind her. 'This won't do.' She tore the plastic
cap off her head and started rubbing the wrinkles and
creases off her face with an energy that bordered on vio-
lence. Turning to the others now gathered in the room,
she shouted, 'Get Derek or Matthew here at once! *Presto!*'

Derek appeared as if from nowhere. 'What is it?' he
asked Daniela coolly. 'What's the problem?'

'It's this girl!' Daniela shouted, pointing at Jennie.
Then with stinging coldness, 'She's incompetent. I will
not let her touch me again!'

Derek took Daniela's arm and looking deeply into her
eyes said a few things softly in Italian. Then he led her
gravely, gently towards the door. At the threshold, he
turned and behind Daniela's back gave Jennie a comforting smile.

Jennie's hands were trembling as she went to work on
her next subject. She continued automatically until an
unmistakable presence at her side made her pulse race.
Derek drew her into a quiet corner of the room.

'Daniela's on the warpath. And she can be a very dangerous woman when aroused, as I know only too well,' he

sighed dramatically, and then looked at Jennie with a wry smile, as if examing her afresh. 'Believe it or not, she's jealous of you. But there's no reason for it, is there, Jennie?' His voice was suddenly low, insistently serious. 'Is there?'

Jennie could feel her heart beating violently beneath her thin dress, making her tongue thick. She wanted to scream her love at him, but no sound emerged from her lips. After what seemed an eternity, he shrugged, 'I've reassured her as to the purely incidental, purely professional, or should I say painterly, nature of our interest in each other.' There was a passing glint of mockery in his eyes. Jennie wasn't sure whether it was real or she had merely imagined it, for his voice now was earnest.

'I've calmed her down. But, Jennie, I'll need your help. A little teamwork, please. Treat her respectfully, gently, reassure her. It's important. Otherwise she may turn this whole film into a disaster.' He squeezed her shoulder, as if to give her courage. But the touch might have been Matthew's. It was one professional talking to another. Jennie rose to the challenge.

'I'll do my best,' she said, avoiding his eyes. She returned to her table, just as Daniela, coffee in hand, came through the door.

Jennie moved into action. 'Come and sit down, Daniela. I'm sorry I was so clumsy before. You were absolutely right to say I was incompetent. That bumpy bus ride must have done something to my hands. But they're steady now, see?' She held her hands in front of Daniela and then with deliberate gentleness began to wash off the remains of the previous make-up job. As Daniela began to relax under her hands, Jennie chatted, told her what a wonderful woman her mother seemed, how delightful Giancarlo was and just like her. She managed to keep her tone easy, sincere, and she could feel Derek's glance clothing her with approval, as if she had passed the test. So this is what's meant by teamwork, she sighed inwardly—all the while keeping up the bubbly chatter, yet wondering whether Daniela was really fooled.

The rest of the day passed uneventfully. There was no further sign of Derek. Daniela seemed calm even at the end of the long day's shooting when Jennie removed her make-up. But it was a calm which made Jennie feel uneasy, as if the storm were to burst at any minute. Even the note from Derek in the hotel pigeonhole did little to stem her unease. 'Thanks, Jennie,' it read, 'you did brilliantly. Keep it up.'

The storm broke the next day and Jennie's efforts could do little to assuage it. Daniela rampaged to the extent that Jennie found it difficult to remember the generous, intelligent woman she had known in London. The thought occurred to her that it was all, of course, an act, and there was no better actress than Daniela when she put her mind to it. And the purpose of that act, it came clear to Jennie in a flash, was to get rid of Jennie. She chuckled bitterly to herself, remembered how she had sensed Daniela's ruthlessness, how Daniela had promised her she would win. And now, without Derek's help, she was powerless. There was no way that a mere make-up girl could triumph over the star.

But where was Derek?

Piero told her that he had left early that morning for Rome with Enrico. They weren't sure when he would return. Jennie shivered. He hadn't even bothered to tell her. So it was all over. Everything was over. It was merely a question of time.

The first ultimatum came that very day. Daniela couldn't bear to have Jennie anywhere near her. She wanted her off the set. Piero tried to reassure Jennie that the mood would pass, but Jennie knew better. She lolled listlessly round the hotel beach for two days. Early on the morning of the third, Matthew asked her if she could give him a few minutes.

Embarrassment evident in his every gesture, he told

her, as kindly as he could, that it would probably be best if she returned to London. Daniela's temper showed no signs of improving and she made it clear that she wanted Jennie away.

'Quite irregular,' Matthew shook his iron-grey head. 'But I've wired the studio to say that you would be coming back. And I've praised your work, so don't worry about that.'

Jennie shrugged. She had expected nothing different. There was a cold deadness in her which seemed to make the worst inevitable. She packed methodically in preparation for the morrow's departure, flinging her white lace skirt in the dustbin. No need for that in London, she thought to herself with a shudder. When Piero knocked to ask if he could take her into Cefalu for a goodbye meal, she acquiesced, forcing herself to be cheerful for him. The effort drained her, and when he kissed her a friendly goodbye at the door, promising to see her when he next came to London, and to write, it was all she could do to smile sadly at him and say how much she looked forward to that.

In the bed next to Kathy's that night, she thought briefly of writing Derek a note. But what could she say? The tears sprang to her eyes. 'I love you, you fool'? 'Goodbye and thanks'? It was all pointless. Suddenly a thought began to form in her mind. Yes, that was it! A portrait—a nude. What better comment on their fleeting relationship. Her fingers itched to begin and she fell asleep, her thoughts full of that golden face as it had gazed passionately on her that single starlit night.

Jennie had several hours to spare before catching her plane the following morning. She spent them, charcoal in hand, doing a nude study of Derek. All her yearning tenderness went into the firm lines of his body, the animal suppleness of his flesh as he reclined on one elbow, his eyes casting a brooding intensity out of the portrait. Jennie felt pleased, and as she threw a last glance at the sketch before placing it in the large envelope she had purchased from reception, a bolt of longing shot through her. She stiffened her shoulders, licked the envelope shut with a little grimace, picked up her bags and marched to reception. As the taxi pulled away from the hotel, she stopped herself turning a backward look on the beach, on Cefalu, the site of so much joy, so much pain.

Back in London a grey mist hung over everything. Jennie's eyes, now used to the Sicilian light, sought in vain for clarity. In a way she was glad—less need to hide. She walked up to her flat, which looked singularly bleak, dumped her bags and went to knock at Mrs Owen's door. The old lady greeted her with oohs and aahs.

'You look quite lovely, my dear—so brown. But aren't you back early?'

Jennie smiled at her evident pleasure in having her back, avoided her question and handed her the small present she had bought at the last minute at the airport.

'You shouldn't have,' Mrs Owen protested, smiles wrething her face. 'But I'm so glad you did,' she chuckled as she tore open the paper to find a pitcher bright with Sicilian colours. 'It's lovely, dear.' She went to put the pitcher on her small mantelpiece. 'It quite transforms the room. Oh, but, Jennie, do tell me about Sicily.'

Jennie sat sipping the tea Mrs Owen had prepared, trying to put excitement in her voice while describing her 'holiday', as the old lady persisted in calling it.

'And what about your young man?' Mrs Owen's eyes crinkled coyly as she passed Jennie what remained of her chocolates.

Jennie almost choked on the soft-centred object in her mouth. 'Not *my* young man,' she said with a touch too much severity in her voice.

'Oh, my dear, I am sorry if I've said the wrong thing,' the old lady looked genuinely dismayed. Then, after a pause, 'Come along, let me help you unpack.'

Jennie accepted gratefully, happy for the company in the flat which gave her no pleasure.

Nothing much did, it seemed, from then on. She reported at the studios the following Monday, was assigned to a new play, a costume drama of the kind she usually loved. But she did her work automatically, finding no satisfaction in it. Even her painting didn't relieve the deadness in her. She couldn't rediscover her passionate commitment, though she continued to dab colour desultorily on canvas, making herself work to pass the time.

The days trailed on, one much like the next. She stopped checking her mail fitfully to see if there might be some word from Derek. Friendly letters from Piero kept her posted on the progress of the film, but told her nothing of what she really wanted to hear. She scanned them for mention of Derek, even of Daniela, but Piero was too high-minded for what would have been tantamount to gossip. She stopped riding her bicycle, began taking the tube to work, somehow pleased to see that its bleak grimness reflected her mood. She was almost relieved when her stepfather turned up one night, just because it broke the monotony. The ghost of Max seemed definitely to have been put to rest. If nothing else, she thought wryly to herself, Derek had certainly changed her in that respect. Her stepfather's appearance no longer had all those dreaded connotations.

One Sunday after she had showered, she took a good look at herself in the mirror. She looked thin, drawn, the colour gone from her cheeks, leaving only an ivory pallor. Pull yourself together, Jennie, she said to her image. It's finished, over. And if it happened once, it might happen again, with someone else. She breathed deeply as if forcing herself to believe it and continued to admonish herself. Work, woman, take an interest in life.

She dressed carefully that day, putting a little colour into her cheeks, and as she caught her reflection in her tall painting glass, she realised that she looked no different than before the tanned self of the sun-filled island—a slender, long-haired girl with dark eyes in a fragile, finely etched face, set off by a belted white blouse and jeans clothing shapely legs.

It's off to life, she chided the image in the glass, bar a certain deadness in the region of the heart. She picked up her sketchpad and went to unlock her bicycle, pumping air into the tyres so that it was usable once again.

A fine drizzle had given way and the sun peeped through the clouds with glimmering freshness. The shy light struck a chord in her. Perhaps it was the simple things one had to focus on, the play of sunlight on a leaf, the sense of one's legs moving. She cycled on, looking at the city in its early Sunday peace. Yes, it was just possible to be alive, despite everything. She pushed the nature of that everything, which had crystallised into Derek's golden image, out of her mind.

Jennie made her way to the park and looked round for Colin. There he was, his dark austere face bent over a sketchpad as if no time had passed. She almost ran towards him.

'Hello, stranger,' he greeted her. 'What? No tan?'

Jennie grimaced, 'It washed away in the shower. I've been back for a while.'

He looked at her questioningly. 'Given up the weekend stint?'

'Only temporarily. I'm back today, as you can see.'

A potential customer approached Colin.

'I'll buy you a drink later, all right?'

'That would be nice.'

Jennie noticed that her chairs were leaning by the railing. She threw Colin a grateful glance. At least *he* hadn't altogether forgotten her.

Jennie set to work. It turned out to be not too bad a day: a few children, a woman, even two rumbustious youths evidently down from Scotland for a football match, who flirted with her outrageously.

When it began to drizzle again, Colin came over to her. 'Shall we call it a day? I want to show you something.'

Jennie nodded.

'A drink first, perhaps—I'm parched!'

They packed up their things and Jennie followed Colin to his van. He lifted her bicycle into the back. 'Let's go and have a drink down by the river close to my place.'

'Yes, all right,' it was Jennie's turn to examine him. His black eyes above the aquiline nose seemed to have a new light in them.

'What's up, Colin? What do you want to show me?'

He chuckled, 'Well, I couldn't hold it back for long. I've got a show coming up, a big one.'

'That's wonderful!' Jennie's voice was warm with congratulation. 'I can't wait to see the work.'

'Very soon now. I think it'll make you laugh.'

Colin's studio was on the Isle of Dogs, a fair trek in the van, which seemed to be held together with Sellotape. They stopped at a little wharfside wine bar and sat looking out on the river, its waters running swiftly grey. Colin bought a bottle of wine and they shared it.

As he poured her a second glass of wine, Colin examined her, stroking his moustache reflectively. 'I don't know, Jennie, but it strikes me there's something wrong. Want to talk about it?'

Jennie demurred, 'Just tired, I guess. Sicily was a bit much.'

He looked at her as if he wanted her to go on.

'I was sent packing by the star.'

'Not that man who once came to see you in the Park?'

Jennie flushed, controlling her voice with difficulty. 'No, he's the writer. She's a rather hot-tempered lady.' An image of Daniela throwing a tantrum suddenly sprang to her mind.

'You haven't lost your job, have you?'

Jennie shook her head. 'No, just on to another project.'

'I see,' but he looked as if the explanation was far from satisfactory.

Jennie changed the subject. 'When do we see these pictures?'

'Now, if you like.' He stood up and they drove the short distance to his studio. It occupied the top floor of a disused warehouse and Colin had somehow managed to make the large dank room into home and workplace all at once. He had built a bed on stilts, beneath which he stored his work. Beside it there was a small round table, a sofa, some chairs and a lovely old stove he had picked up at a jumble sale. One tiny corner of the room served as a kitchen. The rest, opening out to the large windows which gave on to the river, was work space, crammed with plants, canvases, easels, supplies. The walls, Jennie noticed, held none of his work, only a few paintings obviously by friends. It was a good place, she decided, filled with the atmosphere of work. She curled up on to the sofa.

'I'm waiting, breathlessly!' she laughed, the sound feeling quite new in her throat.

He handed her a glass of wine, placed an easel at a little distance from her and perched a large canvas on it.

Jennie caught her breath. There in front of her was the Park, crowded with people, all painted with an absolute regard for detail, and yet all somehow magical. In their midst one figure stood out, a face with large dark eyes bent over a sketchpad. It was her.

'It's wonderful, Colin!' She looked at him, her eyes glowing with admiration.

He chuckled. 'You make an excellent model—so still, so concentrated.' He brought out more canvases. Each one, in one pose or another, had Jennie at its centre.

'I'm honoured,' she said truthfully.

'And I'm grateful. You've got me an exhibition. I feel I should give you one of these—and if you wait patiently until after the show, I will.' He came over to sit by her side. 'I'd love to do you now, in this room, if you'd let me.'

Jennie smiled. 'It will make me intensely uncomfortable. But why not? Though I may not be quite so still as when I'm unaware of you, I warn you.'

'You'll do.' He put a fresh canvas up on the easel and set to work. Jennie sat there, feeling odd but strangely at peace, dreaming a little, not too sure whether she was awake or asleep. Colin's voice brought her out of her reverie.

'Right, that's it for today, madam. The light's giving out. If you'd like to arrange for a sitting next week . . .'

Jennie giggled. 'Do I pay or do you pay me?'

'Let's see how it turns out first, shall we?' he quipped, moving to wash his hands and then coming to sit beside her, his lean legs stretched loosely in front of him. He ran his fingers through her hair.

'I've been wanting to do that for a long time,' he said softly.

Jennie looked at him oddly. He pulled her towards him, searching for her mouth, and kissed her gently. She went through the motions of response, but a tight knot coiled inside her. Little beads of perspiration formed on her skin. At last, feeling nausea mounting in her, she drew away.

'It's no good, Colin, I can't.' There were tears in her eyes.

He trailed a finger along her cheek and she shuddered, suddenly cold.

'You've got that distant look in your eyes again. What is it, Jennie? Is there someone else?'

She shook her head fiercely. 'I'm just hopeless at all this,' she gestured vaguely and got up, needing desperately to move. She looked down at him, sitting huddled in the sofa, his face sad. 'It's not you, Colin,' there was a note of pleading in her voice, 'it's me. I'd . . . I'd like us to be friends.'

He shrugged. 'We are friends, of a kind.' He looked up

at her and took in her distress. 'It's all right, Jennie.' He got up and put his arm around her shoulder, squeezing it. 'Come on, I'll buy you some dinner, now that I'm going to be a rich man—well, a richer man, in any case.'

He took her to a pleasant little Greek restaurant and then drove her home. As he lifted her bicycle out for her, he smiled at her warmly, 'Next week, same time, same place. That's an order!'

Jennie nodded, glad that he wasn't offended. But the yearning ache had returned again, snaking through her like some life-sucking creature. She crawled into the lonely coldness of her sheets, unable now to keep Derek out of her thoughts. Her very blood called out for him. She suddenly remembered Daniela's warning and it rang in her ears with a pounding fatality. 'He will take you over and make you unfit for other men.' Yes, he had taken her over. She could feel his powerful hands now as if they were upon her, bringing her body to life under their firm caress. And then, as Daniela had so sagely predicted, he had dropped her, lost interest, made her unfit for anyone else. She pulled the blanket up, shivering as if its weight were that of a coffin lid buried under snow.

Jennie dragged herself to work the next day, but by lunchtime she felt she must be ill, so leaden were her hands. She begged off and went home, desultorily picking up her post, forcing herself up the stairs. She made herself some tea and toast, took the tray to her bedroom and curled up in bed, trying to bring some warmth into her limbs. Her fingers strayed over the envelopes—bills, adverts, and then an odd one with an Italian stamp. Her heart leaped. She tore the envelope open, her fingers trembling, and read: 'My dear Jennie,

I have been meaning to write to you for some time now, but one thing and another, perhaps my guilt, has prevented me. I treated you very badly and I am sorry. Of course you are not incompetent.'

Jennie read on, her eyes skimming the page rapidly for the name she was looking for.

'I should tell you that Derek and I are not lovers any more. Perhaps it was already dead when I was in London, but I refused to believe it . . . And of course, I was jealous of you. You know, I suppose, that that was the reason for my unprofessional behaviour. I think perhaps he was a little in love with you, even if he did not altogether know it . . . I hope in time you will not think too badly of a silly woman, fearful for her age and looks. I extend my apologies. Perhaps we shall have occasion to meet again in happier circumstances. Daniela Colombi.'

Dear Daniela, Jennie thought, as she read the letter a second time. A tempestuous battler, ruthless when she had made up her mind to it, but fundamentally honest. She wondered whether things might have been different if Daniela hadn't had her sent away, whether Derek might then really have grown to love her. But she didn't let herself pursue the thought. Best to try and forget. After all, if Derek cared for her at all, he would have written, made some sign. It was kind of Daniela to say he had been a little in love with her. Love, what was it? A momentary passion while she was physically present—and then only when his mind wasn't on other things. But no sooner gone than he forgot her. A gust of anger suddenly swept over her. To think that she had almost been ready to give herself to this man! And even now, the filming obviously over—she checked the postmark on Daniela's letter; yes, it was Rome, not Sicily—he still couldn't find the time at least to acknowledge the drawing she had left him, to ask how she was.

Jennie nursed the flame of anger, fanned it into a searing rage. Springing up from her bed, she began aggressively to tidy her flat which she had let decline into an unspeakable state. All the while, she made a mental list of all the things she found hateful about Derek: his cocksureness, his overreaching arrogance, the way he had trifled with her emotions, with Daniela's too; his mistaken assumptions about her which betrayed a fundamental insensitivity.

She scrubbed and polished and swept, and when the flat gleamed, she took out some paper, found a pen and began to write to Daniela. She felt an odd kinship with the woman. After all, they had both been dumped—there was no elegant way of putting it.

'Dear Daniela,' she wrote, 'Please believe I harbour no grudge against you. I understand how you must have felt. But there was really no need. Derek was only playing with me. I hope we'll have a chance to work together in less tense circumstances.'

She went out to post the letter and when she got back, finding nothing else to clean, she pulled out her Sicilian sketchbook. Full of the energy that anger brings, she set to work transforming these visual notes into paintings. She prepared a palette bright with primary colours, akin to the famous Sicilian ceramics, and began to dab aggressively at the canvas.

She worked like a demon for the next few weeks, cycling to the studios, coming home to paint frantically, her energy fed by her rage which was now like a cold steel blade within her. She saw Colin on Sundays and occasionally during the week. Warmed by his friendship, she sought somehow to make her body respond to him. In time, she thought, give it time, though deep inside herself she knew there was only Derek.

She bought herself a new dress for the opening night of the exhibition, a dress bright with blues and purples, reds and greens, like the colours she was putting on her canvases. It dramatically set off the fragility of her features, making her eyes even wider in her face, her skin translucent, her hair raven-bright.

The exhibition night came and she found herself at the centre of an interested crowd. She could hear the whispers. She was the model in the canvases. People came up to

chat to her, complimented her as if she were somehow
responsible for the paintings. She thought at one point
that she detected Max and was almost eager to confront
him with her total indifference. But no, it was someone
else.

One man distinguished himself from the crowd: a tall,
gaunt man with steel-grey eyes beneath a mass of salt-
and-pepper curls. He approached her with the assurance
born of authority and success, his perfectly-tailored suit
falling elegantly over his narrow frame. Eyeing her critically up and down so that she felt like some butterfly
beneath a collector's glass, he said,

'Colin tells me you're an artist as well as a perfect
model.'

Jennie demurred, modest under his gaze. 'I paint, yes,
but an artist . . .' she shrugged her shoulders.

'Let me be the judge of that. Come and see me some
time with a sample of your work.' He handed her a card.
She glanced at it briefly and a surge of excitement went
through her. It bore the name of Dorian Biddell, one of
the best gallery-owners in London.

'I will,' she said tentatively, 'when I'm ready.'

He bowed almost imperceptibly, raised an ironical eyebrow at her obvious hesitation and walked away.

The next day she asked her supervisor whether she
could take two of her holiday weeks soon. They were
granted, and Jennie set up a rigorous routine for herself,
drowning herself in work. She painted with a ferocity she
had never before experienced; forcing herself to leave her
easel only for an imposed daily walk which incorporated
shopping for Mrs Owen.

The summer sun set late outside her window and
when the dark made further work impossible, she
toppled into bed, her dreams filled only with colour.
Once or twice a particular painting would bring Derek
back to her, standing tall in golden light, but she forced
his image aside, relegating it to that knot of anger which

seemed to coil eternally within her.

When her holiday period was over she looked around her room critically, eyeing the canvases she had completed. Not too bad, she thought, trying to be objective. She rang Dorian Biddell and made an appointment to see him. Days at the studio whistled past until the appointed time arrived. Jennie had arranged to have slides taken of what she considered her best canvases and armed with these, a small painting and a bookful of drawings, she approached the gallery. A sense of trepidation suddenly overtook her. If Dorian Biddell was scathing about her work, it would send her back down the slippery path to despair. Perhaps it would be better to carry on just as she was.

Jennie flung her shoulders back, tried a confident smile and strode into the gallery. It was too late to turn back now. She was shown into a little office at the back of the large gallery space. Dorian Biddell sat behind a large desk, warm with the texture of mahogany. He was on the telephone and he gestured for Jennie to sit down. She looked at him from beneath lowered lids. His face beneath the steely grey eyes was severe, but there was a sensuous turn to the mouth, a flare to the nostrils that suggested, Jennie suddenly thought, a cruel sensuality. She sat stiffly, waiting for his conversation to finish.

After what seemed an interminable time he turned to her, his eyes slightly mocking as he took in her obvious nervousness.

'I see you've decided to take up the challenge.' His words seemed to ring with a double significance.

'If you mean the challenge of my work, yes,' Jennie managed a cool reply.

His eyes flickered over her long legs, moving slowly up her body. At last, a gravelly chuckle came from his throat. 'Right, let's have a look at the work, then.' His eyes were amused.

Stiffly she handed him the boxful of slides. He dropped

the slides one by one into a projector that stood on a small table by his desk. 'Anything you'd like to show me before I dim the lights?' His tone was provocative.

Jennie passed him the canvas and sketch book. He took his time, looking at the work critically, saying nothing. His face was serious now. Without a pause, he moved to draw a blind and flicked on the projector. Larger than life, Jennie's paintings appeared on a smooth white wall.

'Give me an idea of scale as we go along,' he said tersely.

As the images focussed on the wall, one by one, Jennie named measurements. When there were no more, he moved to pull up the blind, still saying nothing. Jennie sat tensely, suddenly gripped with an urge to bite her fingernails, like a little girl confronted by an examination.

At last he spoke, his eyes reflective on her face. 'They're good. I would say promising, but they're just a little better than that.'

He buzzed his secretary asking her to bring in some coffee. 'Or something a little stronger, if you'd like?'

Jennie shook her head. 'Coffee would be lovely.' She was still tense, anxious for his final decision, though a small seed of hope was growing in her.

While they waited for coffee, Dorian Biddell made small talk, drawing her out about herself, her education. Finally, when the coffee was before them, he said abruptly, 'Well, I think I can find room for you in a group show in about eight months' time.'

A smile of elation broke over Jennie's face. Six months in the gallery world was like tomorrow.

He returned her smile. 'But before I can make a definite decision, I'll have to see the work face to face. Arrange a date with my secretary on your way out.'

She almost skipped out of the room, not knowing how to thank him.

'Don't thank me,' he said. 'I'll get my cut—and a substantial one at that. In any case,' he let his eyes glide over her again provocatively, 'it's good to meet something more than a pretty face.'

Jennie flushed, thanked him again, arranged an appointment with his coolly blonde secretary and walked out into the street. She suddenly wished she could ring Derek and tell him the news. Somehow, despite everything, she knew it would please him.

Dorian Biddell arrived at her flat promptly at eleven the following Saturday morning. Jennie had tidied up nervously, dressed with care, bought fresh coffee.

'I hope you realise that I don't usually make visits like this on a Saturday morning,' he said by way of greeting. 'But my secretary told me you were busy at work at all other times.' He looked over the small flat critically. 'Haven't you got a man to take care of you so you could devote more time to painting?'

Jennie's cheeks burned. 'I prefer to take care of myself,' she muttered.

'So be it,' he glanced at her ironically. 'But how you expect to make a living out of painting if you have no time to paint . . .' he shook his head in humorous disdain.

She brought in some coffee and biscuits and then began to show him the paintings, standing each on the easel by turn. Again, he said nothing as he looked, carefully now, examining the canvases close up and from a distance. Then he selected five from the series.

'These are the ones we'll show,' he said. 'Have you got any other work I can look at?'

Jennie protested with pleas that it wasn't good enough. But he insisted, and she brought out some earlier canvases.

'That's interesting,' he said, as she accidentally pulled out the painting inspired by Derek, the two floating masks. She made to put it away, but he stopped her, looking at the painting closely. 'Have you done any more in that vein?'

She shook her head, wanting desperately to put the canvas away.

He looked at her reflectively. 'Well, you might consider pursuing it. I wouldn't mind having that one for the gallery's own collection.'

'It's not for sale,' she said tersely.

'I see,' his eyes filled with amusement. 'Oh, these women artists and their love affairs!'

Jennie felt like slapping him hard, but restrained herself and put the canvas roughly back into its place.

'Right. How about letting me buy you some lunch now, and afterwards we can discuss terms.'

'Yes, all right.' Jennie felt a little vague as he ushered her into his sleek Mercedes. Seeing that canvas had suddenly brought Derek into her mind with a jolting intensity. She thought she had mastered his memory, and now, there it all was again, that longing mixed with pain, like an open wound in her side. Would she ever be rid of it?

She forced herself to concentrate on Dorian Biddell's conversation. He was telling her about the other artists she would be showing with. In the midst of it all, he said, 'You might get yourself a telephone, young lady. Leap into the modern world, with your dawning fame.'

'Yes,' Jennie said, embarrassed. 'I've been planning to.'

He took her to an informal little restaurant in Chelsea. 'If you look around, you may spot one or two of your favourite painters.'

Her eyes widened and he laughed, his mouth curling sensuously.

'Come with me to an opening next week and I'll introduce you round,' his eyes danced over her fragile face with its finely etched bones. 'Only, of course, if you promise not to forget who brought you.' He placed a finger under her chin, forcing her to look into his eyes which held an unspoken invitation.

Jennie tried to stop herself from stiffening, but he was

perspicacious enough to notice her response.

'Suit yourself, young lady. But the invitation stands.'

He turned his attention to the menu and they ate. Jennie found herself picking up details about the art world she had never contemplated before. It had a sordidness to it that contradicted all her illusions about the purity of artistic practice, but she knew she would have to face the facts sooner or later. Dorian Biddell was a good teacher and the arrangements he proposed for the sale of her paintings were fair, though in her heart she knew she didn't care. It was the dawning sense of somehow having tumbled into being a professional that excited her. And the excitement fed her almost, though perhaps not quite so much, she realised, as had that cold rage against Derek.

CHAPTER TEN

THE next day was a Sunday and as sunlight streamed into her room around the edges of the curtains, Jennie got up with a lightheartedness which she could barely remember. She hummed to herself as she moved round the flat, brewed coffee and in a celebratory mood, prepared a hot breakfast. I'll take Colin out to lunch, she thought, as she munched crisp strands of bacon and soaked up the gold of her egg with a thick slice of toast. She felt ravenous and the colours on her plate filled her with delight. Finding some dance music on the radio, she all but waltzed out of her flat to knock on Mrs Owen's door. The good news would cheer her. If only Derek had been there to share it with too! She remembered the way he had introduced her as a famous English painter to the Italian woman and stilled a sharp pang which seemed to cut her in half, forcing herself to put the smile back on her face.

'You look like a new person, Jennie,' the old lady said. 'I was beginning to worry about you.'

'I've got an exhibition coming up!' Jennie sang the words and danced the laughing Mrs Owen into her flat to give her a cup of coffee.

Mrs Owen beamed as Jennie filled her in on events. 'I shall take you to the opening personally,' she promised.

'And what a sight I'll make!' Mrs Owen chuckled, preening herself like some young coquette.

Jennie left her drinking coffee and went off to get dressed. No sketching today, no bicycle, she thought, but I'll find Colin in any case. On a whim, she put on the dress she had bought for Colin's opening, matched it with large earring hoops and bangles and feeling like some outlandish gypsy went to show herself off to Mrs Owen.

'You look quite delectable, my dear. Are you off some-where special?'

Jennie giggled, 'Yes, Green Park.'

A knock on the door startled her out of her good humour.

'Oh no!' she breathed. 'Just what I didn't need!'

Sure enough, there stood Harry, looking somewhat the worse for wear.

'I thought I might pay you a Sunday visit.' He looked at her, entreaty in his eyes.

'Come in, Harry.' Jennie tried to keep the irritation out of her voice. Then, with a flash of inspiration, 'I've got to be off, but I'm sure Mrs Owen will be happy to entertain you. There's coffee ready.'

Mrs Owen winked at her. 'Of course I will, my dear. Off with you now and I'll take care of Mr Richards.'

Jennie found Colin in his habitual place. Throwing her arms around him, she told him the good news. 'And I'm taking you off to celebrate,' she tugged playfully at his arm.

'All too ready to comply,' he grinned. 'Where are you going to abduct me to?'

'I haven't the vaguest idea. Let's just stroll and we're bound to find something.'

They did, a jolly little French restaurant where they feasted on juicily tender fillets, paper-thin chips, a bottle of good Macon and more raspberry tart than Jennie could finish.

'Back to the family now,' Jennie grimaced as she sipped the last of her wine.

Colin raised his eyebrows. 'Didn't know you had a family.'

'Don't really. But there's a long-lost stepfather who occasionally turns up and I imagine he's sitting in my flat right now with my dear old neighbour. I left them so I could come and find you.' Jennie marvelled at the ease with which she had come out with all this.

Things had obviously changed in her.

Colin smiled. 'Well, off you go, then. Give me a ring and we can meet during the week.'

Jennie promised she would and made her way slowly homewards on Sunday buses.

She opened the door to her flat, calling out merrily, 'Hello, everyone!' then stopped short. The blood drained out of her face, leaving her dizzy, clinging to the door frame.

'Hello, dear,' Mrs Owen called back. 'Just look who's come to visit!'

On the sofa next to Mrs Owen sat Derek. He rose as Jennie came in. She had forgotten his height, his strong jaw which tensed as he questioned her glance. Her heart set up a mad pounding. She wanted to run from the room, or better still, melt into invisibility against the wall.

He walked towards her, lithe, catlike as ever. Yet his face, under the burnished mass of hair, looked gaunt as he bent to kiss her lightly on the cheek. She clenched her fists, stood taut against him. The clean masculine smell of him rose to her nostrils, making her pulse clamour, exposing her nerves.

'Hello, Jennie,' his voice was low. 'These kind people invited me in to wait for you.'

'Did they?' Her voice bristled. She was suddenly furious at the frenzy he set up in her.

'I came to look for you in the Park—I remembered the Sunday ritual. But you weren't there, so I came along here.'

She glanced at him, so aware of his animal proximity she was unable to trust her voice.

'You're looking very pretty.' His eyes flickered over her and his voice broke huskily.

A nervous hush fell over the room and Mrs Owen stepped in to break it. 'There's some fresh tea, Jennie. Come and sit down here and I'll pour you some.' She rose to give Jennie her place on the sofa. 'I've just been telling Derek the good news about the exhibition, though I couldn't remember the name of the gallery.'

'It's wonderful news, Jennie, I'm so pleased for you. We can celebrate tonight, if you like. I've got the elders' permission.' He smiled at Harry and Mrs Owen.

'You might ask for my permission as well.' Jennie's voice was sharp.

'I promise you the best dinner London can offer.'

'Oh, do go, Jennie,' Mrs Owen burst in before Jennie had a chance to respond. 'I'll take care of Harry.'

'I wouldn't refuse the best dinner in town.' Harry rolled his eyes and rubbed his stomach obscenely.

'I'm not hungry. Perhaps Derek can take you out.'

She could see the glint of anger coming into his eyes. But his voice was controlled and contained a plea.

'Very well, we can go for a walk, dancing if you like. Come on, Jennie, we need to talk.' He directed the full force of his eyes on her.

'I can't imagine what we have to say to each other after all this time.' All the resentment she had nurtured over the last months flashed from her eyes.

Derek took it. 'I deserve that, I guess. I know I've left it rather late, but Jennie, I need to talk to you—alone,' he pre-empted her next remark.

Jennie knew it was a losing battle. She could hear her heart beating wildly, was afraid everyone could.

'I'll be ready in a few minutes,' she managed to say coldly before flouncing into her room.

She leaned against the door, keeping it firmly shut behind her, and breathed deeply. Panic seemed to be rising in her. Now that he was here, what would she do? She couldn't let him set her life askew again. Keep cool, Jen, she counselled her image. And just to show him she didn't care, wasn't impressed by his favours, she decided not to change, only cursorily running a brush through her hair.

'I'm ready,' she announced in a cold voice as she

emerged from her room. She avoided Derek's eyes, and turned instead to Harry.

'Shut the door properly behind you when you go,' she said, hoping he would take the hint and leave her alone for the night, to cry in peace.

Derek's car was parked in front of the block of flats—a silver-grey BMW. Elegant without being ostentatious, Jennie found herself noting randomly.

He slipped in beside her and reached for her hand. She pulled it away jerkily, as if his touch were deadly, and sat as near her door as she could without toppling out.

He grimaced, the muscles in his neck growing taut. 'I deserve that too, I guess. But don't provoke me too far, Jennie.' His voice held a threat.

'And don't use that tone of voice on me, or I'll get out right here!'

He pulled the car from the kerb just as she reached for the handle. Suddenly he laughed throatily. 'Still the same old Jennie!'

'No thanks to you.' Her voice was thick with hostility.

'I don't know,' he threw her an ironical glance. 'Perhaps you should say thanks to me. Unless something has changed in the interim.'

A flush mounted in her face, making her ears ring. Her eyes brimmed poison. 'You arrogant bastard!' the words burst from her.

He chuckled. 'That's what they all say!'

'Well, go to the rest of them, then,' she lashed out at him. 'And leave me alone!' The beating in her head seemed to cloud her eyes and she looked ahead blindly. She could sense his fingers gripping the steering wheel tightly.

'But it's you I want, Jennie,' his voice was almost inaudible when it came, 'with all your deeply guarded secrets.'

She didn't know whether she had heard him or simply imagined his words. She stared fixedly ahead, so keenly aware of his presence that there was no need to look at him. With all her forces mustered against him, she could still feel him drawing her towards him, as if his body were a magnetic pole and she some little fragment of metal clutter.

'Where are you taking me?' she asked at last, her voice coming from a great distance.

'I'm kidnapping you.'

'No one will bother to pay the ransom.'

'I'll collect that in my own way,' he teased.

But she didn't respond, feeling suddenly drained of all energy. Derek parked the car by the side of a leafy square. Children's voices rang merrily from somewhere in its midst. Derek turned to her, and she took in the blue of his eyes, so reminiscent of the sea, and knew her resistance was weakening. He took her hand now and she didn't struggle, simply let it lie there like a tame animal. He stroked her hair, noted the pallor of her face, its almost awesome fragility against the riotous colours of her dress.

'Please, Jennie, be a little patient with me.' His voice was rough with emotion.

She followed him up a few stairs to a handsome wooden door. Her eyes threw him a question.

'It's home—I wanted to show you something.'

The door opened on to a long corridor, panelled in tawny gold pine. Derek led her into a large high-ceilinged sitting room, framed by pine-shuttered windows at either end, and pointing to a soft leather armchair, beckoned her to sit. She sank gratefully into the chair's comfort, watching him discreetly as he poured her a drink. Again she found herself marvelling at the sheer grace of him, that lithe form, the rugged face with its expressive eyes beneath the golden hair. An ache of sheer longing came over her, but she pushed it back, making herself sit up tautly, poised for what was to come.

Catching her eyes on him, Derek returned a look which

sent a shudder through her. He passed her a tall ice-laden glass and raised his.

'To you,' he said simply.

They gazed at each other for a moment, then he reached a hand out and pulled her from her chair.

'Come upstairs.'

She trailed after him, glimpsing objects that she would have liked to handle, noting the few good paintings on the walls, the fine arrangement of contemporary furniture mingled with old. So like him, she thought suddenly. He led her into a booklined room with a large marble fireplace, and Jenny stopped short as she saw what hung over the mantel. Her two sketches of him, beautifully framed and oddly juxtaposed, the sunlit nude and the swaggering he-man.

'You see, I take your image of me seriously, whatever my actions may suggest,' he chuckled, and Jennie found a smile rising to her lips.

'Will the real Mr Hunter please stand up?'

'Which one would you prefer, Jennie?' He was suddenly upon her, his golden face alight with mockery as he crushed his lips brutally to hers, suffocating her. She pummelled his chest hard, forcing her face away, unable to stop hitting him as the rage of months surfaced.

'Right, I gather that's the one you don't like,' he said, laughing. 'Funny, you know, he's quite successful with the ladies.'

Then his face was suddenly transformed into seriousness. He trailed a finger lightly over her cheek, sculpting her features as his eyes grew black with a brooding intensity. He searched for her mouth gently, letting her passion grow to meet his until she felt she couldn't distinguish his lips from her own, her pulsing breath from his.

His face, when he released her, was naked, vulnerable, and her heart leapt out to him. She lowered her eyes, unable to look at him. She wanted desperately to say

something, something which would break the mood, distance her a little from a desire which she felt would too
quickly overwhelm her.

Her voice was ragged as she sought for the right tone.

'And I thought the sketches were meant for your
grandmother!'

He laughed huskily, still holding her to him, 'Only one
of them was, if you remember. And she thought it was
little too risqué.'

'You mean there really is a grandmother?' Jennie
looked at him in astonishment.

'Do you take me for a liar, young lady?' he said sternly.
'I may be many other things—uh-uh, don't bother to list
them—but I am not a liar. If you don't believe me, I
shall prove it to you right now.'

Playfully he pulled her after him, Jennie still not sure
whether to believe him or whether the whole thing was a
jest. They went up another flight of stairs and Derek
pressed a bell.

'Don't worry, I'm not taking you to see a relic,' he
whispered to her, noticing her anxious look. 'Grannie even
manages to travel from the country up here periodically.'

A stout middle-aged lady opened the door.

'Hello, Mrs Woods. We've come to pay a brief visit.
Will you ask Grannie if she can receive us?' He ushered
Jennie in, introduced her to Mrs Woods, and before she
could catch her breath, an imposing elderly woman was
upon them.

Almost as tall as Derek, her grey hair neatly gathered
into a bun, her eyes still a clear blue, she smiled at Derek
warmly and took Jennie into the gesture.

'Hello, Gran. I've brought you a visitor, the one who
draws those naughty pictures.'

Jennie flushed, but the old woman's outstretched hand
and the twinkle in her eyes told her it was unnecessary.

'I've been telling him for years to stop behaving like a
fool, my dear. I'm glad to see someone else has caught

him at it.' Her admiring glance at Derek betrayed her words, but Derek took them up.

'Sh, Gran! I told Jennie you thought of me as an intellectual.' He kissed the old woman on the cheek, led her to a chair and motioned for Jennie to sit down as well.

'Jennie's got an exhibition coming up, Grannie,' he added.

'Well, as long as she doesn't display you. We wouldn't want the world to know,' she bantered to Derek, and then, turning to Jennie, 'That's wonderful, my dear. Where will you be exhibiting?'

Jennie named the gallery.

'That old rogue!' Mrs Hunter laughed. 'Never mind. He runs a good establishment. I hope you'll invite us.'

Jennie assured her that she would and then seeing Derek get up, rose as well.

'Do come and see me again when you have the time, Jennie. Don't wait for my grandson to invite you. He's so busy scurrying round the world, I never see him.'

'You're going to see so much of me for the next few weeks, you'll be happy to have me leave!' He kissed the old lady goodbye warmly.

'There, she's altogether real, isn't she?' he smiled at Jennie once they were down the stairs.

'Yes, and lovely with it.'

'Well, you've obviously made a conquest of her, let alone me.'

Jennie looked at him oddly.

'Yes, me, though you may not know it yet.' The playfulness left his face as he looked at her intently, a little muscle moving tensely in his jaw. She felt her stomach beginning to flutter and she lurched away from him, afraid of his touch.

'I can see I'm going to have a little convincing to do,' he said, his voice rough, 'and a little explaining.' Abruptly he walked away from her.

Jennie shivered. Warmth had gone with him and she

felt very small, very alone, standing there in the long hallway with its single densely green fern. She fingered its leaves abstractedly, sinking into a reverie so that when he returned, she jumped.

'I've booked us a table. I think we have some talking to do. Please, Jennie,' his eyes filled with entreaty, 'don't make it harder than it already is.'

She gazed at him, not understanding, perhaps not wanting to understand; it would draw her into his web again. As if I'd ever been out, she thought, her inner voice filled with scathing self-contempt.

Derek drove skilfully, smoothly through a tangled maze of streets, and Jennie quite lost herself in the process. They stopped by a canal, its darkening waters filled with gaily painted houseboats.

'Quite a different world here,' she noted aloud.

He nodded, helped her out of the car, gripping her arm so tightly that she flinched. He released her with a shrug, folding his hands into his trouser pockets and giving her a wary look. They walked side by side, but apart, towards a small mews restaurant. Jennie noticed the name and gasped.

'But, Derek, that's far too extravagant!' she exclaimed.

'We're celebrating, remember?' he said tersely, and her heart sank as they stepped into the intimate, simply-furnished room.

Unwilling to look at each other, they concentrated on the menu, which was filled with detailed descriptions of the food at hand. Brandade of smoked trout; leek and pumpkin soup thick with cream; guineafowl basted in limes; duck in ginger and honey. The list was small but select. Jennie wished the knot in her stomach would uncoil so that she could enjoy what sounded like exquisite food. She caught Derek's eye.

'If you're thinking what I'm thinking, then we'd better make a pact and be friends for a while,' a slow smile spread over his face, melting her coldness. 'The wine will help. They have some of the best in London.'

He ordered a bottle, and as Jennie took a sip of the mellow fruity liquid, she felt she had never tasted wine before. She answered his expectant look with a wide smile of her own.

'That's better, Jennie.' He took her hand and held it firmly so that she couldn't withdraw. His eyes on her face were warm with tenderness, glowing in the candlelight.

'I'm going to get this over quickly. I'm not good at it, haven't had much practice.' He cleared his throat dramatically, a glimmer of amusement creasing his lips. 'Jennie, how would you like to live with me? Live with me for a long time. I think some people still call it marriage.'

Jennie's eyes opened wide in astonishment.

'Well, it wouldn't be so bad, you know,' he mistook her look. 'I'm not always a brute. My grandmother can vouch for that,' he laughed nervously as she made no response.

'But I thought . . .' Jennie's voice broke.

'You thought what?' Derek pounced at her suddenly.

'Thought you were having a little sun-induced escapade,' she brought it out bluntly.

He looked at her, his eyes grim now as they openly explored her face, her neck, her body, stiff in the upright chair.

'So did I.' His voice was equally blunt.

'Well then?' she challenged him.

'Well then, I was wrong.' He gripped her hand fiercely so that she could feel the indentation of each finger. 'And it's taken me a long time to get used to the idea. I don't plan to get married every day. And when I do, it's for good.'

She baulked. 'You might consider the object of your plans.'

'Oh, Jennie. I'm not doing this very well.' He took a large gulp of wine. 'I've been going through hell,' his voice receded into huskiness and he reached for his glass again. He saw the protest rising to her lips.

'I know, I know, I treated you badly, but I didn't realise

then——' His words trailed off and he forced himself
to continue, attempting matter-of-factness. 'When I got
back from Rome and found your enigmatic drawing, but
not you, Daniela told me you'd taken off because—well,
because I'd abused you. She led me to believe that you'd
had a woman-to-woman chat and that it had all come
out. And she suggested there was someone else. Is there,
Jennie? That Max of yours, perhaps?' He looked at her
defiantly.

She shook her head honestly.

'Good,' he breathed. 'That simplifies things a little. In
any case, when Daniela told me all that, I thought—well,
that's that. I felt only a glimmer of guilt. But it grew, and
when I found out a few days later that Daniela had all
but hunted you off the set, I raged—raged at her like a
real bully. I'm not proud of myself for it.'

He lit a cigarette and looked into Jennie's eyes for some
response. But she said nothing, waiting for him to
continue.

'Well, then . . . oh, the whole thing is too messy, too
complicated. I couldn't destroy the film—a film on which
so many people had worked—simply because I'd behaved
like an idiot. To both of you, I should add. Daniela was
threatening to walk off. I should have finished with her
ages ago instead of letting it trail on.' He shrugged, his
face grim. 'But I like her—like her still,' and he gazed at
Jennie provocatively.

She met him blankly, despite the knot she could feel
coiling inside her. 'Go on,' she said tersely.

'Daniela's good humour was important. Before you left,
she'd already been making a fuss. Do you remember that
day when I came to fetch you at the hospital, and—well,
I was a little distracted, to put it mildly? Not only because
I found you with another man,' a flare of anger leapt into
his eyes only to disappear as quickly as it had come.
'Enrico had asked me to write a film for Daniela based on
an idea I'd had. Daniela had just put her foot down hard

and said she wouldn't work with me again if I was going to carry on with every little bit who caught my fancy. I was dreadfully ashamed of myself for kowtowing to her just to keep her good-tempered. But I was trapped by the situation.'

Jennie's voice broke through stridently. 'And I was just a little bit, as you say. I haven't changed, you know.'

He looked at her fiercely. 'Listen, woman, it's not what *I* said, but what Daniela said. And if you remember . . . Do you remember, Jennie?' He paused, scrutinising her face. 'That's when we went off together, to the temples.'

She gazed up at him, so aware of his harsh masculinity that her limbs turned molten. 'Yes, I remember,' she said, her voice hoarsely low. 'I remembered so well, it almost destroyed my life. I don't want it destroyed again.'

He relaxed his hold on her hand, but kept her eyes riveted on his. The waiter brought their food. The lemon-scented trout tasted like sawdust in Jennie's mouth, and Derek left his plate untouched.

'Jennie, please, listen. I would have written, would have called, but I didn't know what to say, didn't really know the extent of what I felt. But Daniela did, probably knew before I did or she wouldn't have fussed. Well, then I had to go to California and I thought I'd forgotten. But I hadn't. I kept imagining you with that Max creature.' He glared at her, played with the food on his plate and then looked up at her again. 'Jennie, I haven't been able to sleep with another woman since that night in Agrigento.'

A hard laugh rose up in her and burst out.

'You hardly slept with me, if I remember the details precisely.'

'Little bitch,' he murmured under his breath, fixing her with his eyes. 'I was trying to be honourable, trying to spare you. Not that I managed it very urbanely. It's a rule I have. Don't toy with impressionable young women. For all the good it's done me in this case.' He looked at her, suddenly haggard. Yet the edge in his voice persisted. 'But we'll soon change that.'

Jennie could feel his knee searching for hers under the table. She moved her legs away from him, an ironical light suddenly playing in her eye.

'But this time, *I'm* the one who has to agree.'

Derek glowered at her. 'Eat your food, woman, or I won't bring you here again!'

An arch smile flickered over Jennie's face as she obeyed, mockingly demure. She put a slice of guineafowl into her mouth, relishing its exquisite bittersweet flavour. By the time the delicate iced *amaretto* soufflé had arrived, Jennie felt drunk on food. She threw him a deliberately defiant look. 'I think this has been *the* sensual experience of my life.'

He grimaced and then his eyes undressed her, slowly, boldly, catching flame as they travelled over her. 'You have things yet to learn, young woman,' he said, his voice low, carrying both invitation and threat.

'And I intend to choose my teacher through careful research,' she teased.

He scowled at her and abruptly called for the waiter. Having paid the bill, he took her arm roughly and led her towards the car. They drove silently, Jennie trying to make some sense of her inner turmoil, but with no success. Sensing his anger, she didn't dare ask where he was taking her. It was clear all too soon as he pulled up in front of his house and brusquely ushered her in.

He left her alone for a moment and she sat down in the same leather armchair, curling her legs under her. The low pulsing rhythm of piano and bass heralded his return. He had abandoned his jacket and his open-necked shirt moulded the expanse of his chest. Drawing her to her feet, he pulled her into the circle of his arms and slowly, sensuously moved her to the yearning jazz rhythm. Her limbs swayed, glided, blending themselves to his every gesture.

'We're good together,' he whispered into her ear and then, pushing her thick hair back with a gentle stroke, he buried his lips in her neck, sending waves of sensation down her body. With an enormous effort of the will, Jennie pulled away from him. A question had haphazardly risen on the waves of her body and suddenly she had to know the answer. She reached for the packet of cigarettes which lay on the low coffee table and took one, playing for time.

Derek's gaze penetrated her as he watched her movements, and shrugging, he offered her a light. She caught the glint of his eyes in the flame and searched for a cool voice.

'And what are you working on now?' she asked, the sound strange in her own ears.

'I thought I was working on you,' he muttered. 'But obviously I was wrong.'

She pressed on, now resolutely cool, despite his tone. 'Are you doing a new film with Daniela?'

'So that's it!' his face broke into a wide grin. 'Jennie, I may be a fool, but I'm not crass. Or stupid.' He pulled her to him, stubbing out her unsmoked cigarette in an ashtray and lifting her into his arms.

'I'm writing this script about a rather mysterious and beautiful young woman, who has a boozy stepfather hidden in her closet and who wants more than anything else in the world to be a good painter,' he said in mock seriousness as he carried her up the stairs.

Jennie struggled out of his arms and found herself facing him, almost stumbling back into his arms as she sought her balance on the stair. He put out a hand to steady her and looked deeply into her eyes.

'Oh, Jennie, don't. Don't be so defensive. I don't care about the boozy stepfather you're obviously so ashamed of, you haven't even ever mentioned him. I don't frighten that easily, you know. Nor do I care a jot about any of the men you may have known, who've treated you so badly that you seem to be afraid of us all.'

Jennie started to protest, but he stilled her words by placing a finger gently over her lips.

'I care only about you, the you who rises to challenge, who tries to behave honourably, who concentrates intently on her canvases; the you who claims to dislike men and yet kisses me so beautifully . . . so beautifully.'

He pulled her up on to the landing beside him and lowered his lips to hers in a slow searching kiss which made her skin flame.

'You know, you're the only man I've ever been able to touch.' There was a quiver in her voice as she brought it out.

'So that's it,' he said reflectively. He took her hand and guided her up towards the long panelled hallway at the top of the stairs. There, he motioned for her to sit in a plush armchair. A smile hovered round his lips. 'And so it should be, young lady. These things do have something to do with feeling. Perhaps everything to do with feeling,' he added softly. 'So let's stop pretending otherwise, Jennie.'

He lifted her up and held her tightly in his arms, a tenderness mingled with passion suffusing the rugged planes of his face.

Taking it in, Jennie grew suddenly bold. 'And what happens to our mysterious young woman?'

'You'll see,' he said tauntingly.

He opened one of the several doors in the corridor and switched on a light which cast a soft glow over a large room, an enormous velvet-draped bed at its centre. Gently he deposited her on it. His tone still mocking, but his eyes ablaze, he said, 'Got you where I want you at last. And I'm going to keep you here—for good. And love you—all of you.'

With a feather-light touch he kindled her body into flame, and then, his lips against hers, wooing her, crushing her, challenging her into a passion to meet his, he undressed her slowly. Jennie could feel the sea beating in her ears, her body melting into pure sensation, as she ran her fingers over his satin flesh, the firmness of his now bare thighs.

'Oh yes, my darling,' he moaned huskily into her ear, pressing her so fervently to his hardness that his words were like the echo of her own yearning body. And then, suddenly, he lay deathly still. Confusion rose to Jennie's eyes as she caught the glimmer of mockery on his face.

'You haven't said you'd have me yet, haven't agreed . . .' His breath was ragged on her cheek.

'Fool!' She pulled him to her, giving him her mouth, taking in his in a kiss which engulfed them in a single wave. It swept them into a whirlpool of sensuality, a passionate mingling of pleasure and pain, so vibrant with sense and sound that Jennie would never know whether it was her own voice or the throbbing of her blood which had whispered her love.

News about your favourite novels

Send us your name
and address on a postcard
and we'll send you full details
about our forthcoming books.

Send your postcard to:
Mills & Boon Reader Service, Dept H,
P.O. Box 236,
Thornton Road,
Croydon, Surrey
CR9 3RU, England.

Or, if you live in North America, to:
Harlequin Reader Service, Dept. M.B.,
Box 707, Niagara Falls, N.Y. 14302